"Did you feel 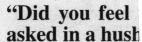 asked in a hush

"Yes," she said in awe. "For the first time."

Strange, but he almost asked if he could feel it too. She must have sensed his desire, because after the slightest hesitation she reached for his hand. "Here." She placed his hand over her belly.

"Just wait. Maybe it will happen again." She covered his hand with hers, and the intimate gesture sent a jagged bolt of desire streaking through him.

This was too personal. He should pull away...

"There—did you feel it?" Her wide eyes met his, eager to share the wondrous experience.

"Yes." The tiny fluttering movements were faint, but distinct. He grinned and kept his hand on her stomach.

"It's a miracle." Her voice was soft, quiet.

"Yes." He gazed down at her and fought the urge to pull her close for a kiss. He tried to hide the husky note of desire in his tone. "So are you."

Laura Iding loved reading as a child, and when she ran out of books she readily made up her own, completing a little detective mini-series when she was twelve. But, despite her aspirations for being an author, her parents insisted she look into a 'real' career. So the summer after she turned thirteen she volunteered as a Candy Striper, and fell in love with nursing. Now, after twenty years of experience in trauma/critical care, she's thrilled to combine her career and her hobby into one—writing Medical Romances™ for Mills & Boon®. Laura lives in the northern part of the United States, and spends all her spare time with her two teenage kids (help!), a daughter and a son, and her husband. Enjoy!

Recent titles by the same author:

THE DOCTOR'S CHRISTMAS PROPOSAL
THE FLIGHT DOCTOR'S ENGAGEMENT
THE CONSULTANT'S HOMECOMING
A PERFECT FATHER

HIS PREGNANT NURSE

BY
LAURA IDING

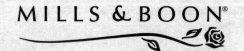

MILLS & BOON®

First published in Great Britain 2007
Harlequin Mills & Boon Limited,
Eton House, 18-24 Paradise Road, Richmond, Surrey TW9 1SR

© Laura Iding 2007

ISBN-13: 978 0 263 85235 6
ISBN-10:   0 263 85235 0

Set in Times Roman 10½ on 12¾ pt
03-0407-42707

Printed and bound in Spain
by Litografia Rosés, S.A., Barcelona

HIS PREGNANT NURSE

To my sister Joan and my brother Michael,
because family is important.
I love you guys.

CHAPTER ONE

CRITICAL Care nurse Caryn Stevens sucked in a breath and tried to squeeze between her patient's bed and the ventilator without success. Her slightly rounded stomach just wouldn't give.

She sighed and moved back around to the other side of her patient's bed where there was less equipment to work around. She was going to have to tell her friends, her co-workers and her boss soon.

Today.

But not yet. Ignoring her early morning nausea wasn't easy but since the entire medical critical care team had just entered her patient's room for morning rounds, she did her best. Especially when she'd waited almost an hour for them to make their way to her side of the unit.

"Good morning, Caryn." Dr. Mitch Reynolds, the critical care attending physician on duty, greeted her warmly. He was engaged to her good friend and ICU nurse Dana Whitney, and she had to admit the two of them made a great couple. Her smile dimmed when she imagined their shocked reaction to her news. "Has Mrs. Nowicki's neuro status improved at all?"

"No, I'm afraid not." Caryn put a discreet hand over her stomach and prayed the meager breakfast she'd eaten would stay down. Nausea wasn't supposed to be a problem this far along. "No response to verbal commands or to light stimuli. Only a decorticate response to pain and even that isn't nearly as strong as it was yesterday."

"Hmm." Mitch turned to his team of eager residents. She didn't recognize any of them—it was the first of the month when the residents rotated to different services.

She dreaded the first of the month.

"Dr. Hamilton, I'd like you to take over the care of this patient now, while I finish the round with the rest of the team. I'm worried about her. I think it's best if we get a stat CT scan of Mrs. Nowicki's brain to see if there are any changes from the one we took two days ago."

"Of course." A tall, dark-haired, breathtakingly handsome man moved out of the group to approach the bedside. He reached for the chart, taking it from Mitch's hands.

Mitch turned to her. "Caryn, have you met Dr. Luke Hamilton? He's the new critical care fellow I recruited from Kansas University Hospital. He just arrived a few weeks ago and this is his first month on the ICU rotation."

"Ah, no, I haven't." Caryn pasted a smile on her face and stepped forward to shake his hand. His grip was firm. Warm. Her instant awareness to his touch was alarming. She took a quick step back. "Welcome to Trinity Medical Center, Dr. Hamilton."

"It's a pleasure to meet you, Caryn." His smile was brief but powerful all the same. "I'm glad to be here. And, please, call me Luke."

She turned away, hiding her irrational reaction to him. "I'd also like to discuss Mrs. Nowicki's nutritional status. Her albumin is still too low and I'm wondering when we can consider feeding her."

"Let's get the scan first before we consider feeding her." Luke opened her patient's chart and began writing orders. Mitch moved on to the next patient, taking the rest of the team with him. "Do I need to call down to Radiology or can I simply write the order?"

Her stomach rolled and she battled the need to vomit. She wished the new fellow would write his orders someplace else and leave her alone. But no such luck. Instead, he looked at her expectantly.

"I think you need to call if you want it stat." Her stomach somersaulted again and she blurted, "Excuse me," and then bolted to the back of the room to the patient's toilet, throwing up the entire contents of her stomach in one sickening lurch.

"Caryn?" Impervious to her acute embarrassment, Luke rushed to her side. His hand was gentle yet strong as he clutched her arm to steady her. "Are you all right?"

No, she wasn't all right. She was pregnant, about five months along, and the baby's father remained in a coma at a local neuro-rehab center since his scuba diving accident nearly five months ago. Her whole life had been turned upside down. How could she be all right?

"Here, maybe you'd better sit down." Luke had

dampened a washcloth and handed it to her, then guided her to a chair. "You must have a touch of flu. It is the season and it's possible you've been exposed by several patients here."

"I just need a minute." Because she felt dizzy, Caryn sat. Thank heavens for baggy scrubs or he would have known she didn't have flu. Still, she wasn't about to tell Dr. Hamilton her problems. So far, she hadn't told anyone her most recent news. Had only, in fact, just figured it out for herself over the past few weeks, confirming her suspicions with a home pregnancy test. The symptoms had been there all along, but she'd been in denial. Big-time denial. "If you want that stat CT scan, you'd better make the call. I'll need to get Mrs. Nowicki packed up to go once they're ready for her."

"Maybe you should go home, get someone else to cover your patients." Luke actually sounded concerned about her.

A hysterical laugh nearly burst free. Go home? He had to be kidding. They were already short-staffed as it was. Besides, she needed the hours since the balance in her savings account was low. Caryn pulled herself together with an effort. Actually, now that she'd been sick, she did feel better. Hungry, even.

Go figure.

"Call Radiology." She desperately wanted him out of her room so she could take care of her patient in peace. Mortifying, to have Luke Hamilton see her at her worst. "The number is on the speed dial on the phones out at the nurses' station."

He hesitated but left her alone. Finally. She pulled herself to her feet then began to document Mrs. Nowicki's vital signs and neuro status, routine, mundane tasks that helped her to get back on track.

When she'd finished, she headed out to the nurses' station. She set the clipboard down next to Luke and pointed to the most recent laboratory readings. "Did you see her sodium level is dropping? And her urine output is very high. Do you want me to increase her fluids?"

"Yes, increase her IV fluids to two-hundred ccs per hour." He wrote the order himself, much to her amazement. She had to admit, whichever nurses had trained him in the past had done a great job. Luke didn't act as if she was there to wait on him hand and foot. In fact, from the little bit she'd seen, he was the epitome of a team player. "Anything else?"

"No, that's all for now." Caryn glanced at the clock. "Is Radiology ready for her?"

"Yes. I'm coming with you."

What? Taken aback, she stared at him. "There's no need. I'm sure you're busy. The residents and fellows don't usually come down on road trips with us."

"Maybe not, but, considering how Dr. Reynolds has entrusted this patient to my care, I'd rather go down with you. I don't feel quite right about her condition. Maybe I'll learn something." He seemed to like that prospect. When she simply stared at him, his grin faded. "Besides, what if you get sick again?"

She winced and glanced around, hoping no one had overheard his remark. His persistence reminded her of a pesky wood tick, stuck to her skin without letting go no matter how hard she tried to shake him loose.

"Fine. Come along then if you must." She stalked off, knowing she was acting childish and ridiculous but unable to help herself.

He followed her, not in the least put off by her attitude. In fact, he seemed in great spirits, looking at the portable monitor with interest.

She gave a resigned sigh. No doubt about it, his constant cheerfulness was grating on her nerves. Or maybe she was just too stressed. She placed a hand over her stomach. So far she hadn't felt the baby move, but then again obstetrics wasn't her strong suit.

She had pulled out her old books from nursing school to refresh her memory. From what she could tell, her pregnancy was progressing normally enough, except for the constant morning nausea. According to what she'd read, the nausea should be gone by now.

"Are you going to throw up again? Would you like me to bring an emesis basin along, just in case?" Luke asked.

"No." She glowered at him and dropped her hand from her belly. "I'm fine."

"I'm glad you're feeling better." He smiled again, the corners of his eyes crinkling in a very attractive way. "I'm anxious to get to know some of the people here, as I'm new to Milwaukee."

"Sure." She couldn't bring herself to smile back. A few years ago she would have been more than a little interested in a guy like Luke. But not any more. She had other, more important things to worry about. Besides, if Luke knew the truth about her condition, he'd be sprinting off in the opposite direction as if his shorts were on fire.

She sighed. This was going to be a really long month.

Luke kept a wary eye on Caryn as they wheeled the patient down the hall to Radiology for the CT scan.

Strangely enough, she didn't look sick; her cheeks were pink without being pale or flushed. Her skin had been warm, not hot, when he'd taken her arm to steady her. Her big brown eyes had seemed a bit exhausted, as if she'd stayed up too late the previous night.

Although his contact with the critical care nurse had been limited, he watched Caryn take care of Mrs. Nowicki and sensed she knew exactly what she was doing, exhausted or not.

He was no stranger to exhaustion. His way of dealing with stress was to bury himself in his work. It was a difficult habit to break.

Maybe it was time for him to get out more, to meet some people and explore the city. There had to be more to life than reading medical journals and patient case histories, right?

"Help me turn so we can get through the doorway," Caryn instructed, leaning her weight against the bed to leverage the turn even as she gave the patient a breath with the ambubag.

The action pulled her scrubs tight against her body and he caught a glimpse of her gently rounded stomach. She was so slim, the bulge seemed decidedly noticeable.

He raised a brow. Was she expecting? If so, pregnancy would certainly explain her upset stomach and the way she kept putting a hand over her stomach. His gaze automatically fell to her left hand and, sure enough, there was a modest diamond ring on her third finger.

A stab of unexpected disappointment assailed him. Stunned at his reaction, he frowned. He shouldn't care if the lovely Caryn was married or engaged. He wasn't looking for anything that even resembled a relationship.

In his experience relationships didn't last—at least, not for long. Better to keep things light and simple from the very beginning.

"This is it." She sent him an exasperated glance, making him realize he hadn't been paying attention. "Honestly, Dr. Hamilton, you don't need to stay down here. I've done this a few times on my own."

Luke liked the way her eyes flashed when she was annoyed. "I'm staying. And I thought you were going to call me Luke?"

She rolled her eyes. "Your charm is wasted on me, Luke."

He kept his tone light. "Can't blame a guy for trying." While the respiratory therapist began setting up the vent, he followed her when she picked up the patient's chart and went into a small anteroom next to the CT scanner. "What does your husband-to-be do, anyway?"

She hesitated and glanced down at her ring, as if surprised to see it on her hand. "I'm not getting married."

She wasn't? "So—that's not an engagement ring?"

"Yes. No. I mean— Like I said, we're not getting

married. Ever." She averted her gaze and focused on the radiology technician who'd just come into the room. "Hi, Greg. How are you?"

The tech smiled. "Good, thanks. Which IV should I use for the contrast?"

"This one here should be fine." She indicated which IV line he should use. Greg injected the dye, then left to prepare for the procedure.

Luke crossed his arms over his chest, raising a brow. "Don't you think you should let the radiologist know about your condition?"

"What condition?" She swung toward him, her eyes wide with alarm.

It was his turn to hesitate. Had he called it wrong? There was no quicker way to alienate a woman than by insinuating she'd gained weight. "The way you were sick earlier, I thought you might be pregnant."

Her jaw dropped and her eyes widened. "You can tell?"

"I am a doctor, you know." He raised a brow when she paled. "What's the matter? Is something wrong?"

"No, but I…uh…haven't exactly told anyone yet." She worried her lower lip between her teeth and he stared for a moment at her mouth.

"I see," he said, but he really didn't. "Is the baby the reason you're not getting married?" He had no business prying into her personal life, but then again as a doctor he was concerned about the welfare of the child.

"Not exactly." She rubbed a hand over her stomach and implored him with her gaze. "Please, don't say anything yet. I need to tell my boss first."

"I won't." Luke hesitated, not liking the way Caryn appeared to be upset over this. The misery in her gaze tugged at him. He reached over to give her hand a quick squeeze. "Hey, don't worry. I promise I won't say a word. But you know, your pregnancy won't be a secret for long." He raked his gaze over her slim figure. "Eventually that small tummy of yours is going to get bigger."

"I know." She held his gaze for a long moment, but then glanced away as if embarrassed. "It's just…things are difficult right now."

He thrust his hands in the pockets of his lab coat and stepped back, reminding himself he wasn't there to get involved. Despite his burning curiosity to know more, he kept his tone bland. "I see."

"No, you probably don't." She grimaced. "To be honest, the father doesn't even know I'm pregnant."

"He doesn't?"

"There was an accident and David suffered a severe brain injury," Caryn continued in a low tone. "He doesn't recognize me or his family." The way she stared down at Mrs. Nowicki's chart sitting in her lap made him want to give her a reassuring hug.

"How long?" he asked, realizing she was in a very difficult situation. No wonder she seemed so alone.

"Nearly five months ago. They're telling me it's doubtful he'll ever wake up." She squared her shoulders and tilted her chin as if daring him to argue. "But truthfully it wouldn't matter if he did. Because, either way, I've already decided to raise this child on my own."

CHAPTER TWO

CARYN didn't know why her life story had tumbled so easily from her lips, especially to a tall, dark, handsome stranger like Luke Hamilton, but she couldn't deny she felt a whole lot better once she'd blurted her secret out loud. Especially when he'd touched her hand, offering support.

It seemed like such a long time since a strong man had held her hand.

Not that she needed a man to be happy, she quickly amended. She looked forward to being independent. Yet being solely responsible for raising this baby was a frightening thought. The accountability and responsibility seemed overwhelming. Despite everything, she'd become very attached to the tiny life growing within her. Late each night she vowed to give her child a safe and secure upbringing.

David wasn't going to wake up. Even if he did, he'd never be the same. She wasn't pining for their relationship, she'd broken off their engagement just before his fateful dive.

Her baby would be fine without a father. She'd do everything in her power to fulfill both roles in her child's life. A happy secure upbringing with one parent had to be a better environment than misery and arguments between two parents.

"Caryn, do you have family or friends to support you?" Luke's blue eyes were filled with concern on her behalf. His unexpected kindness made her want to cry. Had to be the extra abundance of hormones.

"Yes, of course I do." She sniffled and forced a smile. "David's family is very nice."

"So they'll help you with the baby." Luke sounded relieved.

"I suppose, once I tell them the news." She couldn't really speak with conviction because she wasn't sure how they'd react if they knew the truth. She only wore her engagement ring for their benefit.

Secrets. Far too many secrets. They weighed heavily on her conscience.

The heart monitor from the other room set off an alarm and Caryn moved past Luke to attend to it, but he grabbed her arm. "Wait. You can't go out there until they shut the CT scanners down."

Chagrined, Caryn realized Luke was right. Exposure to powerful X-rays were dangerous for the baby without wearing protective lead gear. How could she have forgotten, even for a moment? Luke raised his voice to instruct the radiology technician to shut down the scanner, and as soon as the noise of it stopped, she hurried into the other room.

"Her heart rate is 166 and her blood pressure is way up,

200 over 108." Caryn glanced at Luke, who'd followed her. "I hope this isn't a sign of her brain herniating."

"We need some lasix and mannitol." He looked at the radiology tech. "Do you have any meds down here?"

"Just the emergency medications on the crash cart." The tech looked worried.

"Get the crash cart. I'll call Pharmacy." Caryn headed for the nearest phone.

"Caryn, call a code blue," Luke instructed. "We need more help down here than just the two of us."

He was right. She dialed the emergency number to call a code blue, then the number for the pharmacy, asking for additional medications to be brought to the CT scanner.

Within minutes the room was swarming with additional medical personnel. Therese, one of the other nurses in the ICU, responded as a member of the code team.

"We need to give six milligrams of adenosine," Luke ordered.

"I've got it." Therese was on the side of the patient closest to the crash cart. Caryn didn't care for Therese on a personal level, but she was a decent nurse—when she wanted to be. Emergency situations tended to bring out the best in people.

Caryn held out her hand. "Give it to me—I have her IV on this side."

"OK." Therese handed the medication over. "There's twelve milligrams in the syringe. Give half now and the other half if we need the second dose."

Caryn nodded in understanding as she injected the initial dose of medication into Mrs. Nowicki's IV port.

"Her heart rate isn't responding," Luke observed a long minute later. "Give the second dose, Caryn. Therese, get ready to shock her."

Since the defibrillator was on top of the crash cart next to Therese, the other nurse dialed in the controls, charging up the device in case they needed to use it.

"What did her CT scan show?" Caryn asked, after she gave the second dose of adenosine. "Is her brain injury worse?"

"Good question." Luke glanced at the radiology tech. "How much of the scan was the radiologist able to read?"

"I'll check." The tech dashed from the room.

"Her rhythm looks worse, the QRS is widening, but I still feel a pulse." Caryn glanced at Luke for direction.

"You're right. Please, cardiovert with 25 joules."

Therese gave Luke a private little smile as she dialed in the appropriate amount, then swept her gaze over the patient. "All clear?"

Caryn let go of the IV tubing and stepped back, making sure there was plenty of room between her stomach and the patient as Therese gave the shock. Since the heart rhythm didn't change, Caryn stayed back as Therese deployed another shock.

"Asystole," Caryn said, when Mrs. Nowicki's heart rhythm went straight line, instead of converting into a normal rhythm, as they'd hoped it would.

"Start CPR." Luke turned away when the radiologist came into the room. "Did her scan look worse?"

Caryn had to climb up to kneel on the CT table to perform CPR. After a few minutes Luke came back into the room. When he saw Caryn kneeling at the side of the bed, he frowned.

"Therese, since you're taller than Caryn, would you take over CPR? She looks tired."

Caryn wanted to argue, because she couldn't be tired when she'd just started compressions, but Therese stepped up eagerly. "Of course."

Caryn finished her round of compressions then allowed Therese to take over while she took charge of the crash cart. All too soon, the radiologist returned. He glanced at Luke and shook his head.

Luke sighed, then addressed the rest of the team. "I'm calling an end to this code. Mrs. Nowicki's brain stem herniated and there's nothing more we can do. It's over."

There was a long moment of silence. Then one by one they stopped caring for the patient. The respiratory therapist stopped giving breaths with the ambubag, Caryn turned off the IV pumps and Therese turned off the heart monitor, disconnecting the leads.

Caryn stared down at Mrs. Nowicki, feeling bad about losing her so quickly yet at the same time knowing they'd done everything possible to save her.

The entire situation reminded her sadly of David.

"Thanks for your help, Caryn," Luke said quietly. "You, too, Therese," he added.

Therese responded to his attention like a flower blooming in the sun. "I'm glad I was able to assist," Therese responded coyly. "How lucky you were here to take the team leader role in the code blue, Luke." She beamed at him as if they were the only two people in the room.

The spurt of jealousy toward Therese caught Caryn off guard. What difference did it make if Therese flirted with Luke? Hadn't she learned her lesson with David? Hadn't she decided she was better off alone?

Caryn prepared Mrs. Nowicki for the return trip up to the unit, although urgency was no longer necessary. Luke and Therese would make a striking couple. She turned away, reminding herself that she didn't care. Her future was already set and it included a baby, not a man.

Especially not Luke.

A man as attractive as Luke Hamilton would be nothing but heartache and trouble.

After taking her lunch-break, Caryn stepped into her boss's office. "Michelle? Do you have a minute?"

Michelle Granger looked away from her computer and smiled. "Sure, Caryn. Have a seat. What's up?"

"I, uh, have something to tell you." Caryn edged into the room, feeling inexplicably nervous. She sat in the chair next to Michelle's desk and folded her hands in her lap. "Uh—there's really no easy way to say this. I'm pregnant."

"Oh, Caryn." Michelle's smile was bitter-sweet. Everyone in the unit knew about David's injury. "I'm happy for you, but I'm sure this has been very difficult as well. Are you doing OK?"

She lifted one shoulder. "Yes, still very sick in the mornings for some strange reason, but otherwise fine.

I have my first doctor's appointment the day after tomorrow."

"Do you have any idea when you're due?"

"Early September, I think. But I'm not really sure," Caryn confessed. It was the first of May now so if she'd fallen pregnant some time during their Mexico trip in early December, then early to mid September was probably correct.

"And you're still having morning sickness?" Michelle sounded surprised.

"Yes." Caryn grimaced. "I threw up this morning right in front of Dr. Hamilton, the new critical care fellow."

"Are you taking multivitamins on an empty stomach?" Michelle asked.

She shook her head. "I take my multivitamins with some toast each morning. I just can't stomach a big breakfast so early."

"Try waiting on the vitamins until lunchtime," Michelle advised. Michelle was a single mother and her daughter had just turned five. "Maybe then you'll feel better. And try protein in the mornings—cheese or peanut butter might work. I couldn't take my vitamins first thing in the morning when I was pregnant with Brianna."

Caryn had never thought about the vitamins as being the cause of her nausea, but it was definitely worth a try. "Thanks for the advice."

"No problem." Michelle frowned. "You also might want to go down and talk to someone in Human Resources, Caryn. Since you've already taken a personal leave of absence after your fiancé was injured,

I'm not sure how much time they'll allow you to take off after you deliver your baby. The federal government allows only twelve weeks total in a year."

Twelve weeks total? Caryn stared at her boss in dismay. "But I already took six weeks off when David was injured."

"I know." Michelle's gaze was sympathetic. "I'm sure the hospital will give you at least the first six weeks off work as medical leave, but after that…" She hesitated and shrugged. "I just don't know. I'm willing to grant you personal leave but the hospital administration has to approve it first."

Caryn swallowed hard and slowly stood. "I'll make an appointment with them as soon as possible."

"I'll do whatever I can to help, Caryn," Michelle said softly. "Let me know if you need anything."

"Thanks." Caryn took a deep breath and let it out slowly. "I'd better get back to work."

"Take care."

Caryn left Michelle's office and returned to the unit. The news that she might not get very much time off after having her baby hit like a truckload of bricks. The balance in her savings account was already dangerously low, since the six weeks she'd taken off to be with David had been unpaid. Of course, if she'd known about her pregnancy she would have done things differently. Too bad there hadn't been a crystal ball handy so she could have predicted her future.

She sat in the break room for a moment, so rattled about the news regarding her leave of absence she couldn't think of anything else. Because no matter how wonderful David's family might be, she still needed to support herself.

She needed her full-time job in order to survive.

Luke knew he had a lot to learn during his critical care fellowship and Mitch didn't waste any time in assigning him another couple of sick patients to tend to. They were more than enough to keep him busy yet as the morning went on Caryn became a source of distraction to him. He'd be writing his progress note only to discover his gaze following her as she worked. He didn't understand why the pretty critical care nurse and her baby kept popping into his thoughts.

Although he quickly figured out Caryn had sprung the news about her pregnancy to her boss and probably her friends, too, because the news spread through the unit faster than the speed of light. Soon he overheard bits and pieces of conversations.

"Bet she wishes she hadn't taken that leave of absence to sit with her fiancé all those weeks."

"His family will provide financial support, they're too decent not to."

"Maybe now she'll stop waiting for him to wake up and finally move on with her own life."

The last sentence made him pause. Caryn had emphatically claimed she wasn't getting married, yet apparently that fact hadn't made it through to her co-workers. Why had she kept the truth a secret? Was she worried the medical staff would think less of her for some reason? He couldn't imagine why, given the snippets of conversation he'd overheard.

No, more likely she was simply a private person.

Luke told himself he cared about Caryn's welfare and that of her baby, as any doctor would be concerned about a patient. Maybe Caryn was very different from most women he'd ever known, but that didn't mean he was intrigued by her. Good thing, too, considering she was clearly impervious to his smile.

Your charm is wasted on me, Luke.

He needed to concentrate on his career, which meant keeping his relationships light and tangle-free. His parents had divorced when he'd been very young, and his father had disappeared from his life quickly thereafter. Lisa, his half-sister, had been the product of his mother's second marriage. At last count, his mother had been married five times.

Or was it six?

He wasn't sure why his mother bothered with the hassle of marriage since they never lasted.

A distraught man hurried into the unit and headed for Mrs. Nowicki's room. Her son, no doubt. He'd spoken to him earlier on the phone to break the bad news. Luke watched as Caryn met him at the doorway, immediately putting her arm around his shoulder in comfort, their heads close together as they approached the bedside. After everything she'd been through, he thought it was nothing short of amazing that she was able to give comfort so selflessly to others, even though Mrs. Nowicki's brain injury must have been a difficult reminder of her fiancé.

Struck by the depth of her compassion, he didn't notice how hard he was staring at her until Therese came up beside him.

"Poor Caryn, pregnant and alone."

He wondered if Therese knew how insincere she sounded. He raised a sardonic brow. "Hardly alone. She mentioned her fiancé's family is very nice."

"She told you that?" Therese sounded surprised. "Very interesting, since Caryn usually keeps to herself."

Funny, he'd gotten that same impression. He was suddenly very glad Caryn had chosen him to confide in. "Are you a good friend of Caryn's?"

"Me? Not really, but I can certainly sympathize with her plight." Therese wrinkled her nose. "Except maybe for the pregnancy part—she should have known better than to let that happen. And from what I heard, she's too far along to do anything but have the baby."

Once Luke's attitude would have been similar to Therese's. After all, he'd always taken precautions so he wouldn't end up in a similar predicament. His parents had only gotten married because of him, as his mother had let him know often enough. And then there was the whole situation with his sister. He clenched his jaw, thinking of Lisa's fate.

No one should have to face raising a child all alone, without help. Without support. Without friendship. His gaze sought and found Caryn, still standing beside Mrs. Nowicki's son, giving him all the time and attention he needed.

"Excuse me. I need to give my condolences to Mrs. Nowicki's son." He stepped away from Therese.

Striding toward Caryn, he wasn't at all surprised to see her face was wet with tears she'd shed right along with Geoff Nowicki.

Struck by her caring compassion, he realized in that moment what a wonderful mother she'd make. Her determination to raise her child alone proved she possessed a deep inner strength and commitment. He admired her courage. At the same time he also experienced a strange urge to protect both Caryn and her baby from harm.

He shook off the reaction and focused on his role as a physician. "Geoff Nowicki?" he asked, stepping into the room.

"Yes." The short bald man who was Mrs. Nowicki's son turned toward him.

"Dr. Luke Hamilton. I'm the one who spoke to you on the phone earlier."

"Of course." Geoff Nowicki swiped his eyes on his sleeve and gave Luke a watery smile. "Thanks for everything you did to save her."

"You're welcome, although I'm sorry we couldn't do more." He wished things had turned out differently, but in Mrs. Nowicki's case it simply wasn't meant to be. "Is there something I can do for you? Is there anything else you need?"

"No, thanks. You've been great." Geoff turned and included Caryn. "Both of you. I know everyone did their best for her…" His eyes welled up again and he ducked his head. "Maybe if you'll just give me a few minutes alone?"

"Of course. Take all the time you need." Luke took Caryn's arm so they could leave the room, allowing Geoff time alone with his mother. Tears continued to roll down her cheeks. When they were a few feet away, he glanced down at her in concern. "Are you all right?"

Caryn sniffled loudly but shrugged off his hand. "I'm as fine as anyone who's just lost a patient."

He frowned, sensing false bravado in her tone. "Caryn, you're not just anyone. You're pregnant. And you're in a similar situation. I'm sure Mrs. Nowicki's death couldn't have been easy for you."

Her brown eyes flashed. "You don't know as much about me as you think. I shouldn't have said anything to you about my relationship with David. My personal life is really none of your concern."

She stalked off toward the nurses' station and he let her go. Partially because what she'd said was true, her personal life wasn't his concern. And obviously he couldn't force her to stay.

Caryn would be fine. There was no reason for him to worry about her. She wasn't alone. She had David's parents to help her through this.

He had things to do so he threw his efforts into his work. After checking that all his patients had the medical care they needed and the paperwork was caught up, he prepared to leave, making sure each of the residents understood what they needed to do for the ICU patients in the unit.

When Luke was satisfied that things were under control, he headed home to his downtown condo overlooking Lake Michigan. He'd made plans to go out later with a group of residents who weren't on call, but he was plagued by an uncharacteristic apathy. He couldn't muster the enthusiasm needed to shower and get ready to go out.

He called and canceled his plans then settled in with the latest journal from the Society of Critical Care Medicine. He read the article on severe sepsis twice before realizing he hadn't comprehended half of what he'd read because his thoughts had once more strayed to Caryn.

For a moment, a very brief moment, he allowed himself to wonder what it would be like if her belly was round with his child, instead of someone else's.

CHAPTER THREE

CARYN drove to work the next morning, feeling much better for taking Michelle's advice. She'd nibbled cheese and crackers before leaving the house and didn't feel the least bit nauseous now that she didn't have a huge multivitamin pill rolling around in her stomach.

Although she felt better physically, emotionally she was still a wreck. Last night, after work, she'd gone over to the neuro-rehab center to visit David. His parents had been there, too, like they always were. She'd told them the news about the baby and at first they'd been stunned speechless, then they'd lavished her with attention, thrilled beyond belief with the news of an additional grandchild. Their constant hovering had only seemed to magnify the secrets she'd kept from them until she'd thought she might scream in frustration. In the end, she hadn't even stayed for a full hour before begging off to go home.

She closed her eyes on a wave of guilt. She was an awful person. She'd suspected David was running a fever, but hadn't even asked the nurses about it in her haste to leave.

Caryn pulled into her usual parking space and momentarily rested her head on her hands. She'd thought she'd feel better, telling David's parents at least one of the secrets, but instead it seemed as if telling them about her pregnancy had only caused the other secrets to swell in size as a result.

David's family was very close. They called each other constantly, and from all indications expected to be kept abreast of every pregnancy symptom she experienced. She wouldn't be surprised to discover they intended to go with her to each doctor's appointment and Lamaze class. David's older sister, Debbie, had already volunteered to be her birthing coach.

How could she tell them the truth now?

Very simply, she couldn't.

She had to stop worrying about David's family and start focusing on her future. She'd already met with Human Resources and they were willing to grant her unpaid personal leave after the baby was born.

Which meant she needed to save every dime she could spare, starting now.

Today. There were so many things she needed for the baby, she wasn't even sure where to begin. Yet the knowledge she could make whatever decisions she wanted about her child was liberating.

No more submitting to a man's controlling nature. Ever again.

She headed into the hospital with a renewed spurt of energy. When she entered the unit things were chaotic, alarms going off and a couple of staff members scurrying from bedside to bedside. She'd barely gotten inside the door when one of the night nurses waved her over.

"Help me with this guy, Caryn," Emily called out as she grabbed the patient's arm to prevent him from crawling further out of bed, although his feet were almost on the floor.

She hurried over to get a grip on the patient's other arm and between them they encouraged him to get his legs back into bed. "Wow, you guys must be having a bad night," Caryn commented. "The place looks like a zoo."

"We were two nurses short and it's been like this all night," Emily admitted.

Caryn frowned. "Is there a full moon?"

"I don't know, but it sure feels like it. All the ICUs were short-staffed—there were eighteen sick calls last night."

"Eighteen? For one shift?" Caryn could hardly believe it.

"Hey, you're short-staffed, too. Two of your day shift nurses called in sick."

"Great." Caryn knew some nurses tended to call off sick for the smallest things, but this was ridiculous. "Is there something going around, like some wicked flu bug?"

"I don't know, but your colleagues both called in with severe stomach cramping and diarrhea."

"Lovely. Hope I don't get it." She'd just gotten through her first morning without throwing up—the last thing she needed was some horrible flu virus. Plus she didn't want to waste her sick time, she'd need it for when she had the baby. "Is anyone making phone calls to see if someone is willing to come in and work extra?"

"Not yet. To be honest, we haven't had time." Emily's gaze was apologetic. "The ED has been swamped and we've taken three admissions in the past two hours. I've barely finished the last patient's admission assessment so the most recent admission paperwork hasn't been started."

"I'll take over the new admission if you like. That way you won't need to stay over to finish up." Caryn figured it was a good thing she was feeling better as this was definitely going to be a long day.

"Good." Emily's smile was strained. "He's in bed five. The report I was given from the ED is on the front of the clipboard. All I know is that the patient is thirty-five and received a liver transplant approximately five years ago. He's pretty sick, and no one seems to know what's wrong with him. The critical care fellow is in there, trying to place a pulmonary artery catheter to see if he's septic."

Caryn nodded. "I'll go see if he needs help."

Leaving the confused patient to Emily, she headed over to bed five. She didn't find the whole team in the room, only the resident who'd been up all night and Luke. Mitch had explained how the fellowship program was designed to give additional years of study to specific specialties such as critical care. Luke was technically ranked above the residents, but was not as experienced as the attending physician, Mitch. Still, Luke appeared comfortable working in a critical care unit and was doing fine with placing the catheter.

"Hi, Caryn, you're just in time. I think the tip of the

catheter is in the pulmonary artery. Will you inflate the balloon to see if the catheter will wedge?"

"Of course." She quickly donned a mask and gloves as she'd be close to their sterile field and quickly double checked the catheter's connections, making sure nothing had been missed. She inflated the balloon as he'd asked and they watched the heart monitor for the reading.

"Thanks. Now, while we suture this in place, will you shoot a few cardiac outputs for us?"

She nodded. "I'm getting a cardiac output of 3.1."

"Hmm. A little low. Do you have the rest of the readings handy?" Luke asked, dividing his attention between her and the sutures he was placing to keep the catheter from slipping out of place.

"Systemic vascular resistance is high." Caryn gave him the rest of the hemodynamic readings. One pulmonary artery catheter could give a wealth of detailed information.

"I guess he really is septic." Luke finished with his sutures and stepped back. "Dr. Johannes, place a sterile, transparent dressing over the catheter site, please."

Caryn wrote down all the readings they'd obtained on her patient's clipboard. When she'd finished, she quickly glanced at the report Emily had left for her. The patient's name was Michael Dunn and he'd received a liver transplant five years ago after taking some prescription medication that had caused severe liver toxicity. He'd been in good health until a few days ago.

"Caryn?" Luke called. She glanced up, realizing the procedure was over and the resident, Dr. Johannes, had moved on to write his procedure note, leaving them alone in the room. Luke captured her gaze with his. "How are you feeling?"

"Fine." When he continued to look at her intently, she fought the urge to blush. "Very good," she amended. "Don't worry, I'm not going to throw up on you this morning," she teased.

"I'm not worried," he said in a serious tone. "If you need anything, let me know."

"Thanks." He was sweet to offer his support, but she needed to stand on her own two feet. Literally and figuratively. She gestured to the patient. "What do you think is wrong with Mr. Dunn? Where's the source of his infection?"

"I don't know for sure, but I don't dare stop his immuno-suppressive medications for fear he'll reject his liver." Luke glanced down at her rounded stomach, barely visible beneath her baggy scrubs. "I wish you'd avoid taking care of transplant patients while you're pregnant."

She fought the urge to roll her eyes. "The Center for Disease Control clearly states there's no clinical reason for pregnant women to avoid transplant patients."

He frowned. "But what if you become exposed to a virus we haven't diagnosed yet?"

Caryn knew what Luke meant. Transplant patients were immuno-suppressed, and viruses that were normally innocuous became dangerous to the patient. Pregnancy lowered a woman's immune system, too. "I always use universal precautions."

Luke seemed as if he wanted to argue but just then Dana stepped into the room. "Caryn, we're short-staffed this morning. You can either start the day off with three patients instead of just two or you can be up for the first admission. Your choice."

"I'll take three patients, unless no one else wants to be up for the admission. It doesn't matter. I feel great." Caryn knew her peers were giving her the option because of her pregnancy. She appreciated their concern, but there was no reason she couldn't carry a full load.

"Well, at this point I'll let you be up for the first admission and I'm sure Michelle is going to be asking all of us if we'll be willing to stay for a double. There are lots of sick calls again for second shift."

What was with all the sick calls? "All right, I'll see how I feel. I could probably work a double shift."

"Wait until she's gone through everyone else on the list first," Dana advised. "But thanks. I've assigned Michael Dunn to you in bed five, along with Jerome Hartley in bed six. He's another new admission from the night shift. He has a bleeding ulcer and the trauma team is on the way to evaluate him for possible surgery."

Talk about a busy day. "All right. Thanks, Dana."

"I don't think working a double shift in your condition is a good idea."

She glanced at Luke in surprise, having forgotten he was still there. "Why not?"

"I'm sure you've been under enough stress, without adding more. You need to think about your baby's well-being."

Caryn wasn't going to explain how working a double shift would help get her out of debt so she could afford time off after the baby's birth. And the longer she stood there, the more irritated she became. "I'm sure there are pregnant doctors who end up working long hours. Would you accuse them of not caring about their baby's well-being?"

He grimaced. "I'm sorry, I didn't mean to insinuate you didn't care about your baby, but, Caryn, volunteering for a double shift is very different than working one out of necessity."

"Look around, Luke." She waved a hand at the patient lying in the bed. "These patients are sick. They deserve to have nurses taking care of them." Caryn placed her hands on her hips. "Working a double shift is a necessity. Someone needs to do it."

"But that someone doesn't need to be you."

His stubborn, misguided concern was simultaneously heart-warming and annoying. Thankfully, there wasn't time to argue any further because just then the trauma team arrived to examine her patient with the bleeding ulcer. She quickly headed over.

So did Luke. She tried to ignore his presence as she discussed the patient's care with the team, but she was more aware of him standing beside her than she wanted to be.

Not just because he was a good doctor, but on a personal level.

She briefly closed her eyes, wishing just for a moment that things were different. That she was free to explore these tingly feelings Luke caused.

But she wouldn't trade her pregnancy for anything.

She had to keep her priorities straight. Her baby would always come first.

A guy like Luke wasn't even in the running.

Luke found himself keeping a close eye on Caryn, along with the rest of the ICU patients as the day progressed. Luckily, he was busy enough that he didn't have to see Caryn much. He knew he'd made her angry, but darn it, he wished she'd take better care of herself.

"Luke?" Caryn's voice pierced the din. "I need you to come and look at Mr. Dunn."

He strode over to bed five. "What's the problem?"

"His temperature has spiked to 104 degrees Fahrenheit and his blood pressure is hanging in the low nineties systolic."

No doubt about it, Michael Dunn's sepsis was getting worse. "Have you drawn all the cultures I ordered earlier?"

"Yes."

"Even the special viral samples I asked for?"

"All of them. I sent dozens of blood tubes to the lab." She placed a reassuring hand on the patient's arm. "I've also placed a cooling mattress under him, too, but so far nothing has helped. His fever is sky high."

A sick helplessness washed over him. Losing two patients in two days was a bit much to swallow on his first fellowship rotation in the ICU. "All right, let's start a vasopressor to get his blood pressure up."

"What medication do you want me to start with?"

"Dopamine." He stood at Michael Dunn's bedside and racked his brain for some way to treat his infection, as the treatments they'd started weren't working. Caryn left to get the medication he'd ordered and a second IV pump. She was calm despite the impending medical crisis and he was secretly glad this sick patient was in her care. While she primed the IV tubing, he took the chart and wrote the orders so Caryn wouldn't have to.

"If we need a second vasopressor, start neosynephrine." He added more orders to the chart. "And I'd like him to start on antifungal medication, too."

"All right." She took the chart from his hands and her fingers lightly brushed his. The shock was electric, zapping his hand as if he'd touched a live wire. The way her gaze darted to his told him she felt it, too. Then she quickly averted her gaze, signed off the orders and tore the second ply out of the chart so she could send it to Pharmacy.

He watched her retreating figure as she left the room. The sexual awareness between them wasn't just his overactive imagination. He'd never met a woman he was more in tune with. Yet Caryn seemed determined to ignore the sensation.

A wise move. He should be so smart. He didn't do relationships, although reminding himself of that didn't seem to help keep his eyes from straying to her. She was off-limits, especially considering her pregnancy, and the sooner he figured that out the better off he'd be.

He pushed the uncomfortable thought from his mind and looked back down at Michael Dunn. He didn't know what else to do for the patient. Maybe Mitch might have a better idea.

His ideas sure didn't seem to be getting him anywhere.

"Luke?" Caryn dashed back into the room, working quickly to hang the second vasopressor on the IV pole and priming the tubing. "My other patient is on his way back from surgery. I need you to help keep an eye on Michael Dunn."

"I can do that." He had to bite his tongue to keep from telling her to sit down and take it easy. The morning had gone by surprisingly fast and he'd kept the sicker of the patients for himself, leaving the residents to take over the others. Everyone had been busy, though, as all the patients seemed to be getting worse instead of better.

"I'm turning this on at a very low dose, but I'd like you to stay here for a few minutes to watch his blood pressure. Hopefully, I'll be back soon."

He nodded. "Do you want me to turn up the dose?"

"Only if the blood pressure doesn't respond." Caryn flashed him a tired smile and he was surprised to discover she didn't look in the least bit exhausted. Like most ICU nurses, she seemed to thrive on intense activity. "I'll be right back." She hurried to the room next door.

Only when Michael Dunn's condition had stabilized and she'd gotten her second patient settled in from surgery did Caryn say anything about taking a lunch-break. In fact, Luke was trying to think of a subtle way to suggest he buy her lunch when Dana came over and insisted on covering Caryn's patients so she could leave.

"I won't be long," Caryn promised the petite brunette nurse. "I'll grab a sandwich and eat in the back room."

"Just make sure you have enough to eat," Dana admonished. "I'm sure your baby is hungry."

Caryn laughed and the way her whole face lit up kicked him in the chest, stealing his breath.

She was so beautiful.

She needed to laugh more often.

Luke toyed with the idea of joining Caryn for lunch, but couldn't grab a sandwich for himself until he'd consulted with Mitch on what to do for Michael Dunn. Once he was done, he headed downstairs to the cafeteria to get some food and rushed back up to the small nurses' lounge, hoping Caryn wouldn't mind sharing a meal with him.

When he walked in he found her sitting on the sofa with her feet propped up on the table, her hand on the small swell of her abdomen and a dreamy expression on her face.

Drawn to her as if pulled by some invisible force, he approached. "Caryn?"

"Hi, Luke." Her smile dazzled him. He set his lunch on the table and sat beside her.

"Did you feel the baby move?" he asked in a hushed tone.

"Yes," she said in awe. "For the first time."

Strange, but he almost asked if he could feel it, too. She must have sensed his desire because after the slightest hesitation she reached for his hand. "Here." She placed his hand over her belly.

The simple touch shouldn't have been a turn-on, but it was. Her skin was warm even through the thin fabric of her scrubs and he gently brushed his fingertips over the soft yet firm curve of her belly.

"Just wait, maybe it will happen again." She covered his hand with hers and the intimate gesture sent a jagged bolt of desire streaking through him.

This was too personal. He should pull away. Except he managed to catch a whiff of her strawberry shampoo, which made him want to lean closer to inhale her scent more deeply. Caryn had run around the entire morning between her busy patients but she didn't look like it. A tiny fluttering movement under his palm caught him off-guard.

"There, did you feel it?" Her wide eyes met his, eager to share the wondrous experience.

"Yes." The tiny fluttering movements were faint but distinct. He grinned and kept his hand on her stomach.

"It's a miracle." Her voice was soft, quiet.

"Yes." He gazed down at her and fought the urge to pull her close for a kiss. He tried to hide the husky note of desire in his tone. "So are you."

CHAPTER FOUR

CARYN'S heart tap-danced in her chest, and she couldn't break away from Luke's mesmerizing gaze. "Me?"

He gave her a wry smile. "I've never met anyone so open, so honest."

She desperately wanted to believe him, but she must be making more out of this than she should. Why would Luke bother charming a pregnant woman? And what about her decision to put the baby first? She pulled away. "Then you must be hanging around the wrong kind of women."

"Maybe." He frowned a little when she stood and gathered her paper wrappers together from her rushed lunch. "You still have time to rest with your feet up."

There was that protectiveness again. She was annoyed to discover how vulnerable she was to his attentive concern. "I'm fine, the other nurses need to take their lunch-breaks, too. They were kind enough to let me go first."

He continued to watch her, even as she took her bottle of multivitamins from her purse and swallowed one. "Have you seen the doctor yet?"

"Tomorrow morning." She couldn't wait. At first she'd been worried about not feeling the baby move, but now those fears had been laid to rest. "I'm off tomorrow, which is why I agreed to work a double shift today. My appointment isn't until eleven so I have plenty of time to sleep in."

"Which doctor are you seeing?"

She didn't understand why he cared one way or the other. "Dr. Kingsley. She was recommended by a friend." Serena had nothing but praise for Dr. Marion Kingsley and Caryn hadn't hesitated to use Serena's name to get a quicker appointment.

"Dr. Kingsley has a practice at Trinity Medical Center?"

"Yes. My insurance covers any physician working here at Trinity."

Luke rose to his feet and she noticed he hadn't touched his lunch, which was still sitting on the table. "If you need any help, Caryn, please, let me know."

Help? Like what kind of help? She frowned. "That's a very kind offer, Luke, but I'm fine. Excuse me but I should get back to work. Other people need to get a lunch-break, too."

This time he didn't say anything more when she left the break room.

Caryn returned to her patients, but throughout the rest of the day the memory of sharing her baby's first movements with Luke returned to her at odd moments.

Maybe Luke had handed her a well-practiced line, claiming she was like a miracle. The sad realization was that she'd never felt that sort of special connection before with any other man. Certainly not with David.

Only with Luke.

She was halfway through her second shift when Jerome Hartley, her patient with the ulcer, started to bleed.

Caryn poked her head out of the room and caught the attention of the unit clerk on duty. "Betty, call the critical care resident on call. Tell him Mr. Hartley is bleeding again."

The alarm on the monitor above the patient's head began to sound in response to his very low blood pressure. Caryn reached over and opened the clamp of his first IV so that the fluid flowed wide open, then did the same thing with his second IV. His blood pressure remained in the low eighties systolic.

Hurrying out to the nearest phone, she called the lab. "I need four units of the PRBCs that you have on hold for Jerome Hartley sent to the ICU stat."

She hung up the phone and took a quick moment to check on her other patient, Michael Dunn. She'd finally gotten his temperature down to 101 but she had a feeling it wouldn't stay there. He wasn't due for any other medications for a while yet. Since there wasn't any more she could do for him, she returned to Jerome Hartley's room.

"What's going on?"

Caryn blinked, surprised to find Luke standing behind her. It was already eight o'clock at night and she'd figured he'd gone home a long time ago.

"Bright red blood is pouring out of his nasogastric

tube." She gestured to the half-full canister on the wall. "Just started a few minutes ago."

Luke glanced up at the monitor. "Is his arterial line accurate?"

"Yes. His blood pressure is low, I've already opened up both IV fluids and ordered up all four units of packed cells from the blood bank."

"Good." He smiled, although he looked about as exhausted as she felt. Working a double shift had turned out to be more difficult than she'd imagined. Or maybe she'd just underestimated the physical effects of her pregnancy. She felt like she could sleep for a week. "I'm going to call the trauma team, I think they need to take him back to the OR."

Caryn agreed. Surgery was the only thing that would stop his constant bleeding. She was busy hanging the first two units of blood when the trauma resident arrived.

"I don't think he's stable enough for surgery," the female resident said when she saw the blood pouring through his nasogastric tube.

Was she kidding? If they waited for him to stop bleeding, he'd be dead. With a frown, Caryn continued to monitor the blood transfusion, fully expecting Luke to turn on the charm. Instead, he simply spun around and went to the nearest phone. She listened as he requested the trauma attending surgeon to be paged.

She had to grin at how he'd gone straight to the top. In the time it took the trauma attending to arrive, she'd emptied the blood-filled canister and reconnected the tubing.

"Oh, hell." The trauma attending, Dr. Naomi Horton, took one look at the blood refilling the canister and sighed. "Call the OR," she said to the female resident. "We'll need to take him back as soon as they can get a team in."

The female resident scurried off.

"Thank you." Luke flashed Naomi one of his lethal smiles.

A dimple creased Naomi's cheek. "You're welcome. It's been a bitch of a night and I don't see it ending any time soon."

"I hear you." Luke grimaced. "I'm here because my on-call resident is sick. At least one of my problem patients is now your problem. Let me know when you're finished with surgery and we'll take him back."

"Sounds good." Naomi turned to the female resident. "Are they ready for us?"

"Yes. The team is already here, they've just finished another case." The female resident looked chagrined, as if she knew she'd goofed.

"All right, then, let's go."

Caryn disconnected Jerome from the ICU monitor and reconnected him to the portable one. She helped push his bed out to the elevators, down two floors, then through another hallway until they reached the OR suites.

Since she wasn't dressed in sterile garb, she could only go to the doorway of the room before the OR team took over. "Thanks." Naomi took Jerome's bed and wheeled him the rest of the way inside.

Caryn didn't take offense when the OR door closed in her face. Grateful that something was being done to stop Jerome's bleeding, she turned around to go back upstairs. When she returned to the ICU, Luke met her at the door. He wasn't smiling.

"Take ten, Caryn. You've been running around long enough."

She gritted her teeth and brushed past him, ignoring the way her feet were practically weeping for a break. "Not until I've checked on Mr. Dunn."

No surprise to discover he followed her into the room. One look at Michael Dunn's monitor made her stomach sink. "See? I knew his temp was climbing. It's back up to 104."

"Are any of his culture results back yet?" Luke asked.

"No."

"How many doses of the antifungal meds did you give him?"

Caryn thought back. "Only one, but he's due for another dose now." She winced as she glanced at her watch. "Actually, it was due twenty minutes ago."

She half expected him to yell or at least look annoyed, but he didn't.

"Do you want me to run and get it for you?"

She wanted to laugh. Never had a resident or fellow tried to be so helpful. "Not unless you have access to the pharmacy computer." Which she knew full well the doctors didn't.

He shook his head.

"I'll get it." She left the room and went to fetch the antifungal medication, along with another anti-pyretic for Michael Dunn's fever.

Once things were under control Caryn did take a few minutes to slip into the lounge, even though she could see everyone else in the unit was still pretty busy. She sank onto the sofa and put her feet up on the table, almost whimpering in relief.

"I bought you a present."

Her eyes flew open. Surprised, she saw Luke standing there, holding a wrapped gift. "You did? Why?"

His lips quirked in a smile. "Does there need to be a reason?"

"Generally, yes."

"OK. When's your birthday?"

She flushed, wishing she'd just kept her mouth shut. "Not for a while yet," she answered vaguely.

He set the present on her lap. "Happy pre-birthday, Caryn."

The gift touched her and for a long moment she could only stare at the beautifully wrapped package. Then slowly, prolonging the anticipation, she loosened the tape and removed the pink and blue striped paper.

Luke's gift was a glossy book, entitled *What to Expect When Expecting.*

How sweet. She fought unexpected tears, which had to be hormonal since she wasn't prone to weeping. "Thank you," she said in a husky tone. "I love it."

"I'm glad." Luke looked pleased, then he quirked a brow. "Although you might want to read chapter three, where it talks about how expectant mothers need more rest."

She rolled her eyes. "Stop it. You're acting as if I'm incapable of taking care of myself."

"You're very capable, Caryn." His voice had dropped and despite her best efforts to remain unaffected by his charm, she felt her pulse race. He reached out and lightly stroked her hand. "And very beautiful."

She'd swear her heart stopped in her chest, before doubling its rhythm. Then she grew angry. "Why are you doing this?"

He actually looked confused. "What?"

"Flirting with me." She clutched the book protectively to her chest and rose to her feet, keeping as much distance between them as possible. "I'm sure a woman like Therese or perhaps even Naomi, who is single by the way, are more your style."

"Caryn, I'm sorry. I didn't mean to make you angry." He stood, too, and thrust his hands deep in the pockets of his lab coat. "But is it flirting when I simply state the truth?"

"Yes. No." She let out her breath is a sigh. "Just leave me alone, all right? I have enough problems, without adding your meaningless flirtation to the list."

When he didn't respond with a catchy come-back, she figured he'd finally gotten the message.

Yet when she returned to work, hovering over Michael Dunn's bedside, she couldn't help but wish she hadn't come down on him so hard. Because despite how confused he'd made her feel, she wouldn't have minded keeping Luke as a friend.

* * *

Luke watched Caryn walk away, her words reverberating through his head.

I have enough problems, without adding your meaningless flirtation to the list.

He wanted to call her back, to explain how he really hadn't been flirting with her. At least, not consciously. He was drawn to Caryn by a force he couldn't explain. Not just because she was pregnant and in need of emotional support. But because he liked her. Respected her.

He especially liked spending time with her.

He sat heavily on the sofa and tunneled his fingers through his hair. Maybe he had flirted a little—what normal red-blooded male wouldn't be attracted to Caryn? She was beautiful. Warm. Compassionate. Sexy as hell.

Whoa, where did that thought come from?

Since when did he consider pregnant women sexy? Since…never. He gave his head a quick shake, as if to knock the thought loose. Caryn was right, the dark-haired Dr. Naomi Horton was more his type. But although he thought she was pretty, and a very talented surgeon, he wasn't the least bit tempted to get to know her on a personal level.

Not the way he was intrigued by Caryn.

What was wrong with him? Maybe Caryn's pregnancy was a contributing factor after all. She'd been sick the other morning and looked exhausted now. He couldn't help but think that if she belonged to him, he wouldn't allow her to work so hard. She deserved to be pampered. Standing for hours on her feet, lifting heavy patients, couldn't be good for her or for the baby.

But as she'd pointed out, her personal life was none of his business. She didn't belong to him. What had she said? She'd rather be independent. She planned to raise this baby alone.

She didn't want or need his help.

He sighed and stood. Obviously he was more tired than he'd realized to get so tied in knots over a woman. His day had started very early when he'd been called in to help with the pulmonary artery catheter placement at four-thirty in the morning. Then when he'd been ready to leave for the day, his on-call resident had gone home sick. Luckily, Mitch had arranged for another resident to cover and the guy should be there in about an hour. Luke needed to make sure everything was well controlled by then.

At least, his patients needed to be under good medical control.

He couldn't vouch for his personal life, which seemed to have taken a nosedive with his recent move to Milwaukee. This was supposed to be a new start for him, but he was quickly falling into his old habits of working too hard.

At times like this he missed his younger sister more than ever. Lisa had had a great way of making him see the funny side of life. He missed her laughter.

He stared at the wall, knowing logically he couldn't do anything to bring Lisa back. He had to stop obsessing over things outside his control.

Maybe what he needed was to get out. To try to meet people, have a little fun.

What did Caryn do for fun? As soon as the thought hit him, he grimaced. What was wrong with him? It wasn't like him to obsess over a woman. Especially one that screamed relationship in capital letters.

Somehow he needed to get over his strange attraction for Caryn, and soon.

CHAPTER FIVE

LUKE finished his shift late on Friday, but was determined to get out of his condo anyway.

A group of residents, fellows and attending physicians were all meeting at a restaurant downtown called Andrea's. When he arrived the place was packed with people in a wide variety of age ranges.

Many of them women. He smiled as one of his residents introduced him to a group of very attractive ladies, one of them a lawyer, the second a vice president for a local marketing firm and the third a pharmacist.

He decided Andrea's was a great place, and not just because the food was good. As the night wore on, he lost track of the number of people he'd met. He enjoyed himself, mingling with the crowd, but he couldn't quite stop searching the faces around him for a familiar honey-blonde with a heart-shaped face and big brown eyes.

"How are you doing, Luke?" Mitch asked, clapping him on the back.

"Great." He smiled at Mitch. "Where's Dana?" He hadn't realized until recently that his boss had asked the pretty nurse to marry him at Christmas. He'd overheard Dana telling someone about their wedding, planned for the fall, and seeing the two of them together, so obviously in love, he couldn't dredge up his usual cynical attitude toward marriage. Maybe theirs would be one of the exceptions to the rule.

For their sake, he sure hoped so.

"In the restroom. She'll be out in a minute."

Luke's eyes widened when he saw both Caryn and Dana making their way through the crowd. When the women reached them, Dana stood on her toes and kissed Mitch.

"Hi, Mitch, Luke." Caryn glanced around and he had the impression it was a ploy to avoid looking directly at him. "Wow. I can't believe how packed this place is."

"Can I get you something to drink?" he asked, lowering his head to Caryn's ear so she could hear over the din.

"No, thanks. I'll get it." She turned, as if to make her way to the bar.

"Caryn." He put a hand on her arm to stop her. "Please, let me get you something." When she hesitated again, he added, "I'm sure if Mitch was offering you'd accept."

Her cheeks turned red, as if realizing she was pushing the need to be independent a little too far. "All right. I'll have a ginger ale."

He grinned and held up his half-full glass. "Good choice. That's what I'm having."

A genuine smile curved her lips and he had to stop himself from leaning over to kiss her. He purchased two more soft drinks, handing one to her. Mitch and Dana were deep in conversation beside them. Although the bar was crowded with people, the world had narrowed to include just him and Caryn.

No one else mattered.

"Cheers." He tipped his glass and touched hers, capturing her gaze over the rim.

She tilted her head to the side. "What are we drinking to?"

To us. Luckily, he caught himself before he blurted his thoughts out loud. "How about we drink to new friends?" he amended.

She nodded slowly. "I'd like that. To friendship." She took a sip of her ginger ale. Her moist lips were tempting beyond belief.

"Caryn, do you mind if I ask you a personal question?"

Someone bumped into her from behind and he slid a hand around her waist to steady her. He was glad when she didn't immediately pull away. "I guess it depends on the question," she admitted.

Fair enough. "Why are you so determined to raise your baby alone?"

She stared at him for a long minute. "It's not so much that I want to raise the baby alone, but I don't want to be in a situation where I'm dependent on someone else."

"Because you don't want to get hurt?" he probed.

She shrugged, but the flash in her eyes told him he'd hit the center of the bull's-eye. "Maybe in some ways that's true. But it's more than that. I may not have planned to get pregnant, but now that I am I want to make sure my child is raised in a loving home. A stable, steady environment."

"I understand." And he thought he did. Although he couldn't help adding, "You're smart enough to know that accepting a helping hand on occasion doesn't mean giving up on that loving home or the stable, steady environment."

She frowned a little, as if troubled by that. "Yes."

"Caryn." He lifted a hand to gently cup her face. "I'd like to help, if you'll let me."

Time hung suspended between them as she stared up at him.

Her lips parted, and, unable to help himself, he lowered his head to kiss her.

"Caryn? Is that you?"

She jerked away and he turned in time to see three women making their way through the crowd toward them. He frowned, relieved yet irritated with the interruption.

"Yes. It's me." Caryn's greeting was less than enthusiastic as she turned to the women. "Luke, I'd like to introduce you to Virginia, David's mom, Debbie, David's sister, and Renee, David's sister-in-law." She eased back, putting space between them. "Ladies, this is Dr. Luke Hamilton, one of our new critical care fellows at Trinity Medical Center."

Confused thoughts whirling around his head, he managed a smile as he greeted the women.

"What are you doing here?" Caryn asked them.

Debbie raised a brow. "I was going to ask you the same thing. We came from the theater across the street. We had tickets to see that new musical."

"I've heard great things about it," Caryn said with a smile.

When it looked like Caryn was going to be grilled about her presence at Andrea's he quickly interrupted, offering to buy them something to drink.

"Sure, I'll have a Chardonnay," Debbie agreed. The other women placed similar orders so Luke put the round on his tab and then handed out the drinks as the bartender served them.

There was an awkward pause but Dana came to the rescue, joining the group as soon as she noticed the new arrivals. "Caryn, are you off work again tomorrow?"

She nodded. "Yes, but I work Sunday."

"Well, don't answer your phone," Dana advised. "The sick calls have been coming in like crazy, I've never seen anything like it."

"Lots of the residents have been sick, too," Luke added. "Must be a virus going around. The ED has been jammed with patients all week. Luckily, lots of them just need to be rehydrated before being discharged."

"How have you been feeling, Caryn?" Virginia asked with genuine concern.

"Great." She put a hand over her stomach. "We're both fine."

"You look as if you're not gaining enough weight." Virginia's tone was critical.

For the first time Luke noticed Caryn wore maternity clothes that seemed awfully big, dwarfing her small frame. He hoped the baby was growing the way it should. "Caryn, how was your doctor's appointment yesterday?"

He realized his mistake when Caryn's eyes widened in alarm. At the same time Debbie and Virginia exchanged shocked looks.

"You had your first doctor's appointment?" Debbie exclaimed. "Why didn't you tell me? I would have gone with you. What did he say?"

Caryn swallowed hard and Luke sent her a silent apology with his gaze. She gave him faint smile, and then seemed to gather the remnants of her courage to explain. "My doctor is Marion Kingsley, a she, not a he. And she said I'm fine, very healthy and probably due early September."

"Are they going to do an ultrasound?" Virginia asked, her voice excited. "I just know you're carrying David's son."

"She suggested an ultrasound, but I haven't decided yet," Caryn hedged. She quickly finished her ginger ale. "Speaking of the baby, I need to get home, I'm pretty tired."

Luke wished very badly he could ask Caryn to stay, at least long enough for him to apologize for opening his big mouth, but within minutes Caryn said her goodbyes and walked outside, with David's family close on her heels.

It was all he could do not to go after her.

Once Caryn was gone, he lost interest in sticking around himself. The night was young and the place was still hopping, but he didn't care. Making his excuses to Dana and Mitch, he left.

He stood outside in the cool night air and took several

deep breaths. So much for attempting to forget his attraction to Caryn. Hell, he'd almost kissed her right in front of her former fiancé's family.

Becoming involved with Caryn was scary. Because he didn't want to hurt her.

Yet even knowing that, he didn't think he could stay away.

His gut clenched. Either way, it was a no-win situation.

Physically exhausted, Caryn stumbled up the few steps leading into her tiny bungalow and let herself in with her key. After she'd washed her face and climbed into bed, though, sleep eluded her.

The tiny fluttering movements were back, and she put a hand over her rounded tummy and wished she could share the wonder with someone.

With Luke.

She'd known there'd be a good chance she'd run into him at Andrea's, it was a popular place for the hospital crowd. But seeing him in the casual atmosphere had only complicated things more. Somehow he'd made her feel like the most beautiful woman in the world, despite being five months pregnant.

And for a charged moment she'd suspected he'd been about to kiss her. Until David's family had shown up.

Despite her best efforts, Caryn knew she'd somehow betrayed her instinctive attraction to Luke, because both Virginia and Debbie had bombarded her with ballistic missiles disguised as innocent questions once they'd gotten outside.

"How long has Luke worked in your ICU?"

"Do you work closely together?"

"Is he married?"

"How often do you see him?"

"How did he find out about your doctor's appointment?"

Caryn suspected the last question was at the heart of the problem. Finding out how she'd told Luke about her first doctor's appointment had rankled.

She stared blindly at the ceiling, knowing it was useless to wish things could be different. As much as she was physically attracted to Luke, she had to put the needs of her baby first. A helping hand was fine, but she suspected Luke wanted to offer more. She didn't need anything. Hadn't both Renee and Debbie loaned her a whole bag of maternity clothes? Maybe they were a little too big for her but at least she was saving money on that.

She closed her eyes and tried to think about practical things. But instead her mind continued to relive the moment she'd sensed Luke had been about to kiss her.

The next morning Caryn's phone rang, as Dana had predicted. Not quite as early as she'd expected, though, the clock read eight o'clock as she grabbed the phone.

"Hello?"

"Caryn? It's Michelle. I'm sorry to call so early, but I'm really desperate for help. Will you come in, just for a few hours? Please?"

Her body wanted to refuse but she couldn't ignore Michelle's plea. Plus the extra money, overtime no less, would be an added benefit. "Sure. Give me an hour and I'll be there."

"You got it. Thanks a million, Caryn."

Caryn actually made it to work in less than her estimated hour, as the early morning rush-hour traffic had already thinned out. When she arrived in the unit she was surprised to see Luke. Wasn't he supposed to be off?

She didn't get a chance to talk to him right away, though, because the place was extremely busy. Michelle hadn't been lying. In fact, her boss was wearing a scrub jacket over her work clothes so she could pitch in to help.

After a few hours Caryn headed into the break room to gulp down a large cup of apple juice. When she turned around, she discovered Luke had followed her in.

"Hi." She smiled, and her resolve to stay away evaporated in the secret thrill of seeing him.

"Caryn." He stepped close and rubbed his thumb lightly beneath her eye. "You look tired. Didn't you sleep well last night?"

"Not really." Her cheeks went warm in response to his touch.

"Neither did I." His smile was crooked. "Maybe we could get together for lunch later?"

Instead of refusing, she found herself nodding in agreement. "I'd like that."

"Great." His pager went off and he reached for it with a grimace. "There's another potential admission in the ED. I need to go and evaluate her for myself."

"I understand," she murmured as he hurried off.

She didn't exactly have time to sit around either, so

she returned to her patient care. As she worked, she couldn't help but anticipate her lunch with Luke.

Within minutes, Michelle poked her head into her patient's room. "Caryn, I know you already have two patients, but we're getting a new admission up from the ED. Will you help with the admission? I'll keep an eye on your patients for you."

"Sure." Caryn couldn't argue about the workload, not when she'd never seen her boss look more frazzled. "This is Michael Dunn, he's a liver transplant from about five years ago. He's septic, although we haven't gotten any positive cultures on him to pinpoint the source of his sepsis."

"Unusual for the cultures to take so long," Michelle said with a frown.

"We just can't figure out what's wrong with him. Plus he's had non-stop diarrhea since his admission. We've sent that for cultures, too, but haven't found anything." Caryn washed her hands in the sink. "What's the new admission?"

"An elderly woman with severe dehydration and electrolyte imbalance. I think she's having some heart trouble as a result."

Caryn nodded and crossed over to the only empty bedside in the unit. She'd barely gotten the room ready when Luke brought up her patient.

"This is Mrs. Whalen," he said as she connected the patient to the bedside monitor. "We've given her one liter of fluid in the ED so far. She needs more but we can't give it too fast."

"What was her latest potassium?" Caryn asked when she saw the premature beats on Mrs. Whalen's EKG.

"Still low at 2.8. Twenty milliequivilants are hanging."

"Only twenty?" Caryn was surprised.

"She only has a peripheral line." Luke glanced at her. "When you're ready, I'll need your help to set up for a central line. Once we have that in place, we can give concentrated electrolytes."

"Sounds good." She finished doing her baseline set of vital signs then quickly wrote them on her flow sheet. "Do I have time to do a full admission assessment?"

Luke shook his head. "No, I'd really like to get the line in. I don't like the looks of her rhythm."

Caryn couldn't blame him. She didn't like the looks of her patient's EKG either. The poor woman was almost ninety and looked so frail lying in the bed, hardly aware of what was going on around her.

She went out to get the necessary equipment then helped Luke set up a sterile field around the subclavian site. She donned a mask and sterile gloves herself as there wasn't a resident around to assist.

"I can't believe the sick calls are still coming in droves." Caryn held up the bottle of lidocaine so that Luke could draw some into a syringe.

"Yeah, so much for our respective days off, huh?" He fell silent as he gently inserted the needle under Mrs. Whalen's skin and injected the local anesthetic to help numb the site.

The monitor let off a triple beep and Caryn glanced up in time to see the patient go into V-tach.

"Get me a crash cart," she yelled, shoving the tray of sterile supplies away with her foot.

"Here." Michelle wheeled it in.

"Get ready to shock her," Luke said. Then he frowned. "Wait a minute, doesn't that look like Torsades?"

Caryn had already ripped open the defibrillator pads to place them on Mrs. Whalen's chest. She stared at the monitor for a minute, seeing the way the V-tach grew larger then smaller in amplitude. "You're right. It is Torsades de pointes." Which changed their treatment plan significantly.

Luke nodded. "Get the pharmacist up here with two grams of magnesium," he said to Michelle, who ran to do as he'd asked. "Caryn, we can still shock her, but without the magnesium we may not be able to convert her."

"Do you want me to do CPR instead?" Caryn asked.

He hesitated. "Let's try a series of shocks, just in case. Then we'll do CPR until the pharmacist brings the magnesium."

Caryn attached the hands-free pads then charged up the defibrillator. They'd just completed the three sets of shocks when the pharmacist arrived, short of breath but with the necessary magnesium sulfate.

Abandoning the defibrillator, Caryn quickly gave the bolus of medication. They watched for almost a full minute before the patient converted back into normal sinus rhythm.

"Whew." Caryn took a deep breath and pushed the crash cart out of the way. "That was close."

"You're not kidding." Luke frowned. "Maybe I should have given her magnesium before waiting to start the central line."

"Don't second-guess yourself," Caryn cautioned. "You made the best decision with the information you had at the time. Besides, she needed additional electrolytes, other than just magnesium. The central line was critical."

"I guess you're right." Luke dragged his hand over his face. "Thanks. I needed to hear that."

She couldn't help but smile. It was nice to be able to offer support to him after the things he'd done for her. "You're welcome. Ready to place that catheter now?"

Once the central venous catheter was placed, she turned to Luke. "What caused her to become so dehydrated anyway?"

"The same flu bug everyone else has."

"Not a flu bug after all," Michelle said in a weary tone from the doorway.

Caryn looked up. "What do you mean?"

"We just got a call from the department of health and human services. Apparently the Milwaukee public water system has been contaminated. All these sick calls aren't simply because of the flu, people are sick because they're infected with *Cryptosporidium*."

Caryn felt her jaw drop as the magnitude of what her boss was saying sank in. "You're kidding."

"I wish." Michelle sighed. "It gets worse. We had a record number of sick calls today, sixty-four to be exact with possibly more still to come. Our hospital administrators have just declared a state of emergency because so many staff members have called in sick."

Her stomach sank. "What exactly does that mean?"

"It's just like a snow emergency. All the staff who are currently here are required to stay inhouse. Indefinitely."

CHAPTER SIX

"*CRYPTO?*" Luke stared at the woman in the doorway. He didn't know her name, but she had to be the ICU manager as she wore street clothes beneath her scrub jacket. "The Milwaukee water system is infected with *Crypto?*"

"Yes." The woman raised a hand to rub her temple, as if she had a headache. "And our entire medical center uses Milwaukee water."

"It's not filtered?" Luke's fingers tightened into fists at his side, unable to believe what he was hearing.

"It is in some areas, like in all the ICUs, the OR, the oncology and transplant units. But the rest…" She shrugged.

The enormity of the situation was staggering. No wonder there had been so many sick staff members and patients. His gaze swung to Caryn. "What about you? How are you feeling?"

"So far, I'm good." But her hand was splayed over her abdomen as if to protect her baby. "I have filtered water at home," she confessed. "Not that I'm good about changing the filters."

He gave a silent prayer of thanks that Caryn wasn't infected. Her pregnancy would have made the risk much higher.

"Caryn, you need to take over your other patients, I have to make phone calls to all the nurses who live outside the Milwaukee area to see if they're willing to come in." The ICU manager shook her head. "This whole situation could get worse before it gets better."

"OK." Caryn snapped her fingers and turned to Luke. "Michael Dunn."

"You're right." Luke immediately figured out what she meant. "He's probably got *Crypto,* too."

"But we sent stool cultures," Caryn said as they both headed directly toward Michael's room.

"They don't routinely check cultures for *Cryptosporidium.*" Luke could have smacked himself for not thinking of this earlier. Diarrhea wasn't a common symptom of sepsis, he should have asked for specific parasite cultures, too.

"Can we treat him?" Caryn asked, keeping her voice low.

"I'm not sure. There's a new drug called nitazoxanide but it's only been tested on patients with normal immune systems." He hesitated then added, "I really need to call Mitch, see what he thinks."

"I understand." Caryn's wide eyes betrayed her anxiety.

He reached over to take her hand in his. She didn't pull away, but clutched him firmly as if she needed this small contact as much as he did. He gave her hand a gentle squeeze, then reluctantly let go. "I'll let you know what Mitch wants to do."

"I'll be here." Caryn smiled at him, then turned to her patient.

Getting a hold of Mitch was easier said than done. After almost ten minutes of waiting for him to answer his page, he finally discovered why. "You're sick, too, aren't you?"

"Oh, yeah." Mitch's voice sounded strained, as if he was in pain. "I heard about the *Crypto* outbreak on the news while I was stuck in the bathroom, experiencing the symptoms firsthand. Good timing, huh?"

Luke wanted to laugh, but didn't think Mitch would appreciate humor at his expense. He got straight to the point of his call. "I need to treat Michael Dunn for *Crypto*. Any suggestions?"

"There's a new drug out called Paromomycin or something like that, specifically for immunosuppressed patients."

"I'll try it." Luke had tons of other questions, but sensed Mitch needed to get off the phone, and fast. "Is there another attending I should call to cover for you?"

"I'm working on it. So far the two I've called have been sick, too." Mitch let out a low groan. "I have to go. I'll call you later."

Luke didn't have a chance to respond before Mitch hung up. For a moment he could only stare at the phone. He was on his own, unless Mitch found someone else to help out.

He swallowed hard and tried not to overreact. Was this how it felt to be an attending physician? Solely responsible for an entire unit full of patients? His gut clenched. If so, he wasn't sure he was ready to be cut loose from his fellowship program. Thank heavens he wasn't totally alone. The critical care nurses, like Caryn, were very knowledgeable in their own right. Working together as a team should help them get through this.

Squaring his shoulders, he took a deep breath and began to prioritize patient care.

Luke waited until Caryn was able to take her dinner break, since their lunch date had been put on hold thanks to the *Crypto* disaster. She wasn't able to leave the unit until six, nine hours after she'd started working that morning.

Not that he was keeping track. All right, maybe he was. He couldn't get past the need to watch over her. Especially since neither one of them were going to be allowed home any time soon.

Had she eaten anything at all? He hoped so.

"How are you holding up?" he asked as they headed down to the hospital cafeteria.

"Pretty good. I'm just glad I don't have any of the symptoms."

He shared her relief. *Crypto* was very contagious. He followed Caryn as she filed through the cafeteria line, choosing from a variety of food. Hospital Administration had announced that all hospital employees and physicians could eat free during the state of emergency so he didn't offer to buy her dinner.

The cafeteria wasn't nearly as crowded as it usually was and he was glad when Caryn chose an isolated table toward the back of the large room, giving them the illusion of privacy.

He held out a chair for her.

"Thanks." Appearing flustered, she sat down.

He took the seat across from her and gestured to her plate. "You must be hungry—you skipped lunch."

"I nibbled on some cheese and crackers to get me through the day." She took a large bite of her roast chicken and rice, closing her eyes in bliss. "I am hungry. It's always nice to eat something I didn't have to cook." She flashed a saucy grin. "Or pay for."

He chuckled, appreciating her good humor. "Good attitude for someone stuck here overnight."

"Tell me about it." She sighed. "They're trying to find call rooms for us to use as sleeping rooms, but there aren't enough for the number of nurses who'll need them."

It was on the tip of his tongue to offer to share with her, but sensed she wouldn't appreciate his generosity. He took a large bite of his own meal, nearly choking on the mouthful when he realized the third finger of her left hand was bare.

He swallowed hard and coughed. Reaching over, he captured her hand in his. "When did you take off your engagement ring?"

She tried to tug her hand away, but he held firm. "This morning. My fingers were swollen and I couldn't get the ring on."

"I see." He stroked her bare fingers, enjoying the feel of her silky skin before letting her pull away. Her cheeks were stained a guilty pink. She wouldn't look at him and, having met a few members of David's family, he wondered if there wasn't more to her story. "Caryn. Is your pregnancy the only reason you aren't wearing your ring?"

"No." Caryn traced imaginary designs in the rice with her fork before finally raising her gaze to his. "If you must know, pregnancy is the excuse I plan to use for David's family. I told you before, things are complicated. I just can't bear to continue wearing the ring."

"Then you shouldn't wear it." This wasn't the first time she'd hinted at the problems with her fiancé prior to the diving accident. A tiny, selfish part of him was glad she didn't seem to be harboring deep feelings for the guy. "I'm sure David's family will understand."

She shook her head, her smile grim. "Not necessarily. But that's my problem, not yours."

"You don't have to face your problems alone, Caryn." His tone was sharper than he'd intended. "I'm here to help you."

She paused, glancing at him. "That's the second, no, the third time you've offered to help me, Luke. Maybe you're just a really nice guy, but I can't stop wondering why. Why have you taken such an inordinate interest in me?"

The food he'd swallowed sat heavy in his stomach. This was what he got for prying into her life, he supposed. He hesitated, unsure of how to respond.

"Is it because you don't have a lot of experience or exposure to pregnant women?" she persisted. "Is that it?"

"That's partially true," he agreed.

She knew he was holding back because she set her fork down and pushed her plate of half-eaten food away. "You know a fair amount about me, Luke, but I know next to nothing about you." A faint smile played along her mouth. "Except that you're a good doctor who used to live in Kansas."

"What do you want to know?" He tried to relax, but it wasn't easy. His past wasn't something he enjoyed talking about. But if telling her about himself would make her finish her dinner, he'd manage to get through it.

"Is your family living in Kansas?" she asked.

"No. My parents are divorced. My father left when I was very young. My mother is remarried now and living abroad."

She frowned a little at that. "No brothers or sisters?"

Not any more. He slowly nodded. "I had a younger half-sister, but she died."

"Oh, Luke." Caryn reached out and covered her hand with hers. "I'm so sorry."

"Yeah, me, too." He liked the way her hand felt on his. "It's been a few years, but sometimes it seems like yesterday."

"I know the feeling. My parents died a few years ago, too." A shadow fell over her eyes. "It's hard to lose the ones you love."

He cleared his throat and squeezed her hand, trying to lighten the mood. "Hey, let's not get maudlin here. Sharing dinner with a beautiful woman should be fun, not sad."

She arched a brow and gently slid her hand from his.

"You say that like we're having a date, instead of taking a quick dinner break in the cafeteria."

"If not for the *Crypto* emergency, we would be on a date."

Now her brows rose higher. "Oh, really? You sound awfully confident. What if I'd declined your invitation to dinner?"

"Why would you?" He spread his hands. "I'm nice, charming, handsome—why would you turn me down?"

His playful arrogance made her laugh. "Gee, maybe because you're so modest? And because we have absolutely nothing in common?"

"How do you know that we don't have anything in common?" He was glad she'd picked up her fork and continued to eat.

"Look at you." She stabbed the air with her fork. "Replace those baggy scrubs with a tux and you'd look more like a model than an overworked physician."

He could tell she wasn't kidding. "My looks don't define who I am."

"Then what does?" Caryn propped her elbows on the table and leaned closer. "You're smart, obviously, or you wouldn't have made it through medical school. Your watch is a Rolex, so I have a feeling you're not hurting for money, which is unusual when you consider most physicians come out of med school with staggering loans." He frowned, realizing she wasn't too far off the mark. "What do we have in common? Nothing, as far as I can tell."

"We both lost someone close to us." He kept his tone

serious, so she'd know he meant every word he said. "We're both smart. We both love working in critical care. We both like the theater." He paused, and then added, "We're both attracted to each other."

She sucked in a quick breath, her eyes meeting his. But she didn't deny it. He was very thankful she didn't deny what was happening between them.

"Luke, I'm *pregnant*." She emphasized the last word as if she carried the plague.

"Caryn, you must know I was attracted to you before I knew about your pregnancy," he pointed out.

She sighed. "For all I know, you're attracted to all women." Her dry tone should have ticked him off.

But he sensed she'd been hurt before. Badly. He shook his head. "No. Just you."

She gave a self-deprecating laugh. "Sure, until the novelty wears off. And I expect that will happen when I'm as big as a house."

The image didn't scare him in the least. But the way she was drawing away from him did. Obviously, he couldn't convince her with mere words. "Are you finished? I'll carry your tray for you."

"Yes." She stood and so did he.

After disposing of their dirty dishes on the tray-line, he fell into step beside her as they walked to the elevator. The doors opened, as if waiting for them.

Thankfully the elevator was empty. When the doors closed behind them, he stepped toward her. "You're special, Caryn," he said in a husky tone. "I hope you realize that."

She opened her mouth but didn't say a word. He gave her plenty of time to protest as he tugged her close and then captured her mouth with his.

For a heart-stopping moment she stiffened against him and he fully expected she'd push him away. Then her mouth softened, opening for him, returning the kiss. His heart thundered in his ears as he explored her mouth, drugged on the taste of her.

The doors opened and he broke off the kiss, gulping deep breaths to calm his racing heart. He was tempted to hit the button again so they could ride the elevator for a while longer.

But Caryn was already pulling away, her brown eyes wide with shock. "This isn't going to work, Luke. I'm sorry."

Before he could stop her, she walked out of the elevator and disappeared into the one place he couldn't follow.

The woman's restroom.

He'd kissed her. Caryn stared at her reflection in the mirror and brushed her fingers against lips that still tingled. Why had he kissed her?

Why had she kissed him back?

Because she couldn't think straight around Luke. He muddled her senses, made her doubt the wisdom of her mission. Just like the night before, at Andrea's, she'd been oblivious to the crowd of people around them, aware only of Luke.

Leaning on his strength, his kindness was too easy. Caryn closed her eyes and pressed her forehead against the cool mirror. She was making the same mistakes all over again. Listening to her heart and her body instead of her brain.

No. She couldn't repeat the mistakes she'd made with David. Because this time more than just her heart was at risk.

The baby moved, as if to remind her of its presence.

She straightened, rubbing a soothing hand over her belly. "We'll be fine by ourselves, you'll see," she whispered.

As much as she was attracted to Luke, she had to be strong enough to resist. She had enough problems in her life, without adding more.

When she arrived back in the unit, Michelle met up with her behind the nurses' station. "Caryn, the environmental service department has located a call room for you." Her boss frowned at the clipboard in her hand. "I think we're going to need to rotate through six-hour shifts."

"I'm fine for now," Caryn protested. The last thing she needed was time alone with her thoughts. "Maybe you should offer the rest period to someone else first?"

"I know you're doing fine, but I'm going to need someone to work the night shift." Michelle tapped her pen on the clipboard. "So far, I only have four nurses who've agreed to come in and we need at least seven."

Caryn glanced around the unit. "There's eight of us here now, we're going to need more than one to take a break now to come back for nights."

"Nine if you count me," Michelle said with a tired smile. "Plus, two of the second-shift nurses didn't come in until much later, so I'm planning on having them stay well into the night shift."

"And what about days tomorrow?" Caryn didn't know how many hours she'd be able to work in a row but, pregnant or not, much more than twelve would be pushing it.

"You're right. I still haven't figured all that out yet."

"Let me see." Caryn thought there had to be a better way. She sat down at the desk and stared at the lists of names Michelle had written in for each shift. "What if everyone worked staggered twelve-hour shifts, but only rested for eight? Wouldn't that help provide extra coverage?"

"I'm not sure." Michelle sat down next to her. "What do you mean?"

"I started at nine, so I work until nine or nine-thirty tonight. The nurses who started their shifts at seven should get to go off earlier. The evening staff nurses should stay until three in the morning, and then the people who've been off since seven could come back at that time." She made a quick diagram, showing how the shifts would overlap. "Basically, we'll work for twelve hours, rest for eight, then work another twelve."

"You know, I think that will work." Michelle took the clipboard from her. "Thanks, Caryn. I guess my brain must be fried."

"Don't worry about it." Caryn glanced at Michelle and suddenly wondered about her daughter. "Who's watching Brianna while you're stuck here?"

"She's with my mother. But when I spoke to her earlier, she was crying, asking me when I'd be home." Michelle's sad smile broke her heart. "It was hard to explain that I really had no idea when I'd be home."

Caryn frowned, realizing one day soon she was going to be in the same situation. Not necessarily locked in the hospital because of a *Crypto* emergency but there were always other disasters. In fact, she often had to stay long after the end of her shift just to finish up the work.

The responsibility of raising her baby alone suddenly overwhelmed her. David's family would probably offer to help out, but the very idea of leaving her baby for such long lengths of time bothered her.

"Don't worry, I'm being silly and sentimental," Michelle said with a smile. "I'm sure Brianna will be fine."

"Of course she will," Caryn replied. But as Michelle left, she didn't move.

There were so many things to worry about. Who would she get to babysit? More importantly, how would she afford costly child-care fees? She didn't want to ask David's parents for help, she should be able to stand on her own two feet. Yet thanks to David, and her own stupidity, her financial situation was a mess. The few months she had before the baby was due might not be enough to turn things around, to dig herself out of debt.

She slammed the door on those negative thoughts, reminding herself that she'd take things one step at a time.

And the first step, she acknowledged with a sigh, was to keep herself focused and on track.

Which meant staying far away from distractions.

Like Luke, who happened to be the biggest distraction of all.

CHAPTER SEVEN

CARYN kept herself busy with patient care in an effort to keep her deepest fears under control. She also did her best to avoid Luke. He must have sensed her need for space because he left her alone, talking to her only out of necessity.

"Caryn?" one of her co-workers called across the unit. "Phone call for you on line two."

She left Michael Dunn's room and crossed to the nurses' station to pick up the phone. "Hi, this is Caryn. May I help you?"

"Caryn?" Her stomach clenched when she recognized Debbie on the other end of the line. "The neuro-rehab center called to tell us David's infected with *Cryptosporidium*."

Despite Debbie's anxiety, she wasn't surprised at the news. The rehab center was located within the Milwaukee limits and no doubt had been hit as hard as they'd been with the *Crypto* outbreak. "Lots of people have been infected, but don't worry, David will be fine."

"Are you sure?" Debbie's tone rose dramatically. "What if his condition gets worse?"

It was on the tip of her tongue to mention that since he was already severely brain injured, his condition couldn't possibly get worse. But she didn't. Thanks to her nursing background, David's family had cast her in the role of medical advocate, helping them negotiate a complex medical system. From the very beginning they'd turned to her for answers.

Which only made the secrets she kept a heavier burden.

"The greatest risk is to his kidneys," she finally admitted to Debbie. The lack of oxygen to all his major organs was a problem but everything, except his brain and his kidneys, had bounced back. "We'll just have to wait and see."

"What questions should I ask?"

She rubbed a hand along her temple. "Ask what his creatinine level is and if he's on any antibiotics that might make his kidney failure worse."

"Creatinine, antibiotics," Debbie repeated. "That's all? Nothing else?"

"That's all." Caryn paused, then added, "Debbie, you realize nothing will fix the damage done to his brain."

Debbie was quiet for a minute. "Yes, I know," she said finally. "Thanks for your help, Caryn."

"You're welcome." Caryn hung up the phone, overwhelmed by helplessness.

"Is David all right?" Luke asked with a frown.

Caryn hunched her shoulders and nodded. "As well as can be expected." She tugged on her scrub pants, which were starting to slip off her belly. She tightened the drawstring and retied the knot.

"Are you all right?" he asked in a low tone.

"Fine," she answered, though she wasn't. The walls were starting to close in on her and she wanted to leave. To get out of the hospital. Now. If only Dana or Serena were there, she very much needed a friend to confide in, to talk to. She took several deep breaths and glanced at her watch. Only another forty-five minutes before her twelve-hour shift was up.

Surely she could hang on that long?

"Caryn, I have a call room assignment for you." Michelle crossed over to where she stood and handed her a key dangling from a small chain. "You're in room B120."

"Thanks." She forced a smile. Michelle didn't have to know she planned to escape outside for a while. Just to take a walk, clear her head.

She slipped her key into the pocket of her scrubs. No one needed to know her plans, she'd be back before anyone realized she was gone.

The claustrophobic feeling didn't fade. If anything, her desire to get out of the building grew sharper than ever with each passing minute.

She gave report to the nurse picking up her patients then slipped into the locker room to get her coat. Despite the mild spring weather, at night the air would be too cool to go without.

She didn't see Luke as she headed out of the ICU, taking the opposite direction from the basement call rooms. Instead of moving toward the main entrance, she took the less used back stairwell to the side exit, uncertain whether or not the security guard on duty would allow her to leave, although she certainly intended to return.

Throwing open the side door, she welcomed the cold blast of air that blew into her face as she stepped into the night.

For several long minutes she just stood, breathing deep, her head tipped back so she could see the stars. Being outside helped a little, but the secrets still swirled in her chest, clamoring to burst free. She began to walk.

Trinity Medical Center was a large medical complex stretching over several hundred acres. But the hospital was also located near a city park in a nice safe residential area so she headed in that direction, crossing the street to the hills beyond.

The roads were noticeably empty and she imagined more than half the population lying in their beds, suffering the effects of contaminated water.

The headlights of a passing car briefly illuminated the area then darkness enveloped her once again.

She preferred the darkness, although she did carry a penlight just in case. Taking a walk like this, without fear of reprisals from David, was liberating. She liked making her own decisions.

Leaving the security of the sidewalk, she climbed the small hill. In the summer the ground would be covered in fresh green grass, but while the snow was completely melted, the ravages of winter had been harsh.

In the dark it was hard to tell the difference between brown grass and mud.

As the peacefulness surrounded her, her thoughts settled on her problems.

What was the worst that could happen if she told David's parents, his brothers and sisters, everyone, the truth? Sure, they'd be upset at first, but they'd get over it. And then she'd be free to move on with her life, leaving this less than happy chapter behind.

She let out a loud snort. Yeah. But her financial troubles wouldn't go away. And David's family might resent her for telling the truth. Didn't her child at least deserve one set of grandparents? Heck, for all she knew, they might choose not to believe her.

They had treated David as the golden son. David, the smart one. David, the man who could do nothing wrong.

The truth would tarnish that image for ever.

The ground beneath her feet sloped downward and she missed a step, causing a sharp zinging pain to shoot through her ankle. With a cry, she went down hard.

Sitting on the damp earth, she grit her teeth against the pain as she massaged her twisted ankle. Stupid. She imagined David's mocking voice, telling her how stupid she'd been to step in a gopher hole.

Glancing around, she realized she'd certainly achieved her objective. She was totally alone in the park. She leaned over and rested her forehead on her bended knee. This was what she got for breaking the rules.

When the dampness soaked through her thin scrub pants, she decided to try and stand. Luckily, the pain had receded quite a bit, so she was able to bear some weight on her ankle.

Thank goodness it wasn't worse. Explaining to Michelle how she'd disobeyed orders and taken a walk only to break her ankle would not have been fun.

Favoring her right foot, she limped over the hill back toward the hospital. The wind against her damp scrubs made her shiver. She pulled the coat tight around her chin.

Her walk may have helped the feeling of claustrophobia, but it didn't help her decide what to do about David's family.

Slowly but surely she reached the brightly lit hospital. Since the side doors were locked, she had no choice but to go in through the main entrance. She flashed her hospital ID badge to the security guard, and then walked toward the elevator, bumping right into Luke.

"Whoa, where did you go?" He stared at her coat and windblown hair with dark disapproval. "You weren't supposed to leave the hospital."

"I took a walk, hardly a big deal." She tried to step around him, but winced at the pressure in her ankle.

"Wait a minute. What happened? You're limping."

"Leave me alone, Luke."

Ignoring her cranky attitude, he knelt at her feet and pushed up the bottom of her scrub pants so he could gently probe the joint. "What happened?" he repeated.

"Nothing." She stared at the top of his bent head, wishing she dared to lean on him. "Took a wrong step and twisted it a little, that's all."

"Hmm." He glanced up at her, his fingers still supporting her ankle. "Doesn't seem too swollen, but maybe we should get a quick X-ray. Don't worry, they'll use a lead apron to protect the baby."

"I don't need an X-ray." His protectiveness grated on her nerves. "It's fine," she said, suddenly exhausted. "I'm sure I'll feel better after a little sleep."

He nodded and rose to his feet. "You're probably right." He held out his arm. "I'll walk you down to your room."

Her first instinct was to refuse his help, her rioting emotions bubbling too close to the surface for comfort.

She needed a friend, someone she could talk to.

And despite her resolve to stay away from him, she was tempted, far too tempted to lean on his strength, spilling all the dark secrets buried deep in her heart.

Caryn was uncharacteristically subdued as they rode the elevators to the basement level call rooms. The last time they'd ridden the elevator together, they'd shared a kiss that had shaken him to the core. Was she remembering those stolen moments, too? Luke glanced at her, but her eyes were dull, tired.

Maybe the pain in her ankle was worse than she'd let on.

The thought of her wandering around outside in the dark at eleven o'clock at night made his stomach tighten. From the streaks of mud on her scrub pants, he assumed she must have fallen when she'd twisted her ankle.

Good thing the damage wasn't worse.

He paused outside his assigned call room. "I have an extra pair of scrub pants you can borrow."

She gave a listless nod. "All right."

He frowned, missing her spunk, her sparkle. Something was bothering her, but he couldn't help if she wouldn't let him in. He unlocked her door and opened it. "Come on in for a minute, I'll get you those scrubs."

"I'll wait here." She stood in the doorway, as if afraid to come inside.

He wanted very badly to take her into his arms, but she needed sleep. He picked up the clean scrub pants and handed them to her. "Caryn, I'm here if you need to talk."

"Thanks." She didn't move, didn't head down to her room, like he'd expected her to. She stared at the scrubs he'd given her. "Maybe we can talk later. I'm sure you're exhausted, just like I am."

"Never too tired to listen," he said honestly. If he thought he could convince her to stay, he'd give it his best shot.

It had to be her decision.

She glanced up at him and their gazes met, clung. Then she stepped forward, entering his room, and he quickly closed the door behind her, hoping she wouldn't change her mind.

He gestured to the bed. "Sit down, put your feet up."

She sat, sweeping a curious gaze over the room, barely big enough for the single chair, the small desk and a twin-sized bed. He tried to put her at ease. "If you're wondering, your room looks just like this one."

"It's not exactly five star, is it?"

He had to laugh. "No."

When she sat gingerly on the edge of his bed, he pulled out the chair so she wouldn't feel as if he'd asked her there for some reason other than to talk.

"Thanks." She sighed and reached down to rub her ankle. "I guess it wasn't too smart, to wander through the park alone."

He lifted her foot off the bed and gently began to massage her ankle. "It's a very safe area. But I'm more interested in why you felt the need to go to the park."

She lifted a shoulder. "I needed some fresh air to clear my head."

"Because you're worried about David?"

He braced himself for her answer, but she shook her head. "No. He's in good hands at the neuro-rehab center."

"Caryn." His hands stilled. "You're not still in love with him, are you?"

There was a moment of silence, then she said, "Would you think less of me if I told you my love for him died a long time ago?"

"No, of course not." But he was curious to know more. "What happened?"

"David and I moved in together last year." She stared into space, as if she were talking more to herself than to him. "He asked me to marry him and I naïvely asked him to move in with me."

"Go on," he encouraged.

"We both worked a fair amount of hours, so we didn't see each other all the time but, looking back now, I can see there were signs all along."

He grew angry on her behalf. "He cheated on you?"

"Not exactly, but close." She took a deep breath, then let it out in a rush. "He was hooked on drugs."

"Drugs?" Surprised, he stared at her. The possibility had never occurred to him.

"Cocaine. I didn't find out for sure, not until we went on the trip to Mexico. I didn't even want to go on the trip with him, because our relationship had been rocky for weeks. But David insisted. He loved to dive, wanted me to learn, too." She gave a harsh laugh. "Of course, little did I know he'd spent all the money I'd taken out in a second mortgage on my house, money I'd set aside in a joint account for our wedding."

He muttered a curse beneath his breath. The guy was scum. Worse than scum.

"I hated diving," she confessed. "I couldn't seem to master the technique. Every time I went down, I panicked. David liked to be in control and didn't like it when I stood up to him. Then I stumbled across his stash of cocaine and totally freaked. We had a huge fight. I told him the marriage was off. He didn't seem to care. I wanted to go home, but couldn't speak Spanish well enough to figure out how to change my flight. We still had two more days of our trip." She shook her head. "Can you believe David actually expected me to go on that last dive with him?"

Based on what she was telling him, he wasn't surprised. "So he went on the dive alone," Luke summarized.

"I'm sure his diving accident was a direct result of his drug abuse," Caryn continued, as if he hadn't spoken. "I know he had drugs in his system before he went down. Something happened, his tanks ran out of oxygen or malfunctioned or something. Here at Trinity the ED doctors automatically screen for drugs on trauma patients, but for some reason they didn't down in Mexico. And by the time he was flown back here it was too late." She toyed with the blanket on his bed. "Far too late for me to say anything."

He sucked in a breath. "His parents don't know?"

She shook her head. "They don't know about our rocky relationship, they don't know I broke off the engagement, they don't know about the money he stole from me, and they don't know about the drugs."

"Why the hell not?" He tried to fight his instinctive anger on her behalf. "They should be forced to pay you back every dime you lost. For heaven's sake, you have a child to support."

"I know. But to ruin his reputation like that…" Her voice trailed off. "I just couldn't do it."

"Who gives a rip about his reputation?" Luke asked in a snide tone. "I don't."

She looked directly at him then. "His family does. And I'm pretty sure there are others here who could care, too. David was a doctor, a resident in the anesthesia program."

David had been a doctor. A resident here at Trinity Medical Center. The news was difficult to grasp. Luke had known a few bad apples during his time in the medical field, but he was always surprised anyone would risk so much for so little.

Yet he didn't care about the guy's reputation. As far as he was concerned, she needed to tell his family the truth.

"I feel so much better now that you know," she confessed softly. "As if someone has lifted a steel-lined cape off my shoulders. I've been keeping this quiet for what seems like for ever."

He couldn't stand to see her so upset. He stood, setting her foot back on the bed. Then went around to join her, the mattress dipping under his weight.

Her eyes flew open in alarm, but he simply put his arm around her shoulders and tugged her close.

"You're amazing," he murmured.

She relaxed against him. "No, I'm not. I should have figured out about the drugs a long time ago. If I had, David might not be lying in that neuro-rehab bed."

"Maybe. And maybe not. He might have hurt you, or the baby." He gently splayed his hand over her abdomen. "I'm glad you're both all right." The fluttering movements were back and he smiled. "Hey, the little guy is active tonight."

"*She's* always active when I'm ready to sleep," Caryn corrected softly. "David's parents think it's a boy, but I'm sure this baby is a girl."

"I hope you're right," he said in a low, husky tone. "Because any daughter of yours is bound to be beautiful."

She reached for his hand, entwined her fingers with his. "Thanks for being so nice, Luke."

His heart hammered in his chest, even as he hid a grimace at her choice of words. Nice? He wasn't exactly feeling nice at the moment. Edgy need had kept him in a constant state of arousal whenever she was near. He'd never had so much practice keeping his needs in check as he had since meeting Caryn. He wanted to beg her to stay, but forced the plea back. "You're welcome."

When she didn't move away, he glanced down at her. Her eyes were heavy lidded, no doubt with pure exhaustion. His heart squeezed. She needed her rest.

"Caryn. I think you'd better go." If she didn't go now, he couldn't be held accountable for his actions. "You obviously need to get some sleep."

"If you don't mind, I'd rather stay."

CHAPTER EIGHT

CARYN held her breath as she stared up at Luke. She wanted him to kiss her again. Like he had in the elevator. And this time she didn't want him to stop.

She wasn't sure where the desperate need came from, but didn't care when he bent toward her. She met his mouth eagerly. Just that quick the kiss morphed from one of offering comfort to something heady. Sensual. Thrilling.

She opened for him, silently asking for more. After the first burst of heat, the long drugging kiss seemed to last for ever.

Yet not nearly long enough.

He pulled her close, changing the angle of his mouth to explore deeper. Never had a simple kiss been so intimate, so arousing.

Desire hummed through every nerve of her body, causing her already sensitive nipples to tighten with anticipation. Before she could blink, he pressed her back against the mattress, his hard frame covering hers.

Welcoming his weight, she locked her arms around his neck and arched against him. His hands greedily explored every curve of her body, from her plumper than normal breasts to the swell of her abdomen.

"Sexy," he murmured between the kisses he lavished upon her face, down her neck, as his hand curved around her breast, his thumb stroking her nipple. "You're so beautiful and sexy. Everything about you is a total turn-on."

Stunned, she gasped when his kisses trailed lower, to the V of her scrub top. She'd never been told she was a total turn-on before, even when she hadn't been pregnant. Had never felt like one either. "I'm not."

"You are." His voice was low, husky. "I want to see you. Touch you." He buried his face between her breasts. "Taste you."

She was shocked at how much she wanted that, too. "Yes."

He went still then lifted his head to gaze down at her intently. She held her breath, her heart quickening in anticipation, but suddenly he raised a hand, drew his thumb along her cheek. "You look tired," he murmured, a tiny frown puckering his brow.

"I'm not," she denied quickly. His kisses had driven all lingering fatigue from her mind.

"Caryn." He whispered her name in a groan and leaned down to kiss her again, as if he couldn't help himself. After a few minutes he raised his head and sighed. "I want you so much, but this isn't smart. You need to sleep. I could be paged at any minute and you're back on duty at five."

There was that annoying protectiveness again. She wanted to be angry with him, but couldn't dredge up the emotion. Instead she felt cherished, humbled by the knowledge her needs were more important than his. The hard evidence of his arousal pressed against her yet he pulled away, tucking her head into the hollow of his shoulder.

"Sleep," he whispered.

"But, I thought…" she didn't know what to say. In her experience, men didn't volunteer to stop at this point.

"Shh, it's all right." His mouth curved in a crooked grin. "I won't die from wanting you. If that were the case, I would have been dead days ago."

She chuckled at that, relaxing against him. Being here with him was nice, and as the exhausting events of the day were catching up with her, she closed her eyes and gave herself over to the comfort of his arms. Breathing deeply, she filled her head with his musky scent…

And slept.

The room was dark when she opened her eyes, except for the luminous dial of the small alarm clock. She'd instinctively woken up at four-thirty in the morning.

Or rather the needs of her body had woken her up, as she very badly needed to use the bathroom. Luke was still sleeping beside her so she took care not to wake him as she slipped from the bed. Her ankle gave a slight twinge, but held her weight.

She gathered the spare set of scrub pants he'd given her from the floor where she must have dropped them. Her fingers closed around her call-room key still in her pocket, reminding her there was a bathroom there for her to use which wouldn't wake him up.

Before leaving, though, she gazed at Luke's handsome face in repose. For a moment she wished he wasn't a doctor. That she'd met him a long time ago, long before she'd met David.

The idea that he could be remotely attracted to her was astounding. The way he'd put her needs before his own was just as amazing. He had more self-control than anyone she'd ever met. Especially as it was obvious she wouldn't have said no.

Her honest thought brought her up short. Caught in the thrill of being desired by Luke had almost made her forget her vow of independence. What was she thinking to get involved in a relationship so soon? She had a baby to take care of, a child that wasn't Luke's.

Her confused thoughts ricocheted through her brain like pinballs as she opened the door to Luke's call room and eased through the opening, blinking in the brightly lit hallway. Feeling like a guilty teenager, she hurried down the hall to her own room. There wasn't time to worry about Luke now. She only had time for the quickest shower known to man before she needed to head up to the ICU.

When she arrived on the unit, she was surprised to find the activity had settled down a bit. Caryn looked at the assignment board to see which second-shift nurse she was slotted to relieve from duty.

She took a two-patient assignment from Barbara, one of the second-shift nurses who started at five. Normally she'd have preferred to take the same patients she'd had earlier, but ended up receiving report on two completely different patients. She didn't complain because there was nothing normal about working during a crisis. Although she longed for a huge mug of coffee to help burn the residual sleep from her eyes, caffeine wasn't an option for the baby so she settled for filtered water, watching with barely concealed envy as the other nurses enjoyed a fresh pot. They offered to make her a pot of decaf, but what was the point? Without caffeine, coffee didn't taste half as good.

She'd just finished her initial assessments of both patients when she overheard the on-call resident's one-sided conversation outside her room.

"How far along? And you're absolutely sure she needs to be intubated? Okay, I understand, but this is a decision my fellow needs to make. I'll call you right back." He hung up the phone and immediately began dialing again.

"What's going on?" Curiosity got the better of her. "What decision?"

"There's a pregnant woman in the ED having seizures because she's in full-blown eclampsia. They've already intubated her and started her on continuous infusion of magnesium sulfate. They want to admit her here in the ICU to deliver her baby."

"What? Why?" The phone rang and he jumped to it, explaining the whole thing to Luke. The details didn't sound any more reassuring the second time around.

"OK, I'll meet you down there." The resident hung up the phone. "Get ready, because Dr. Hamilton agreed to admit the patient here."

"But we don't deliver babies in the ICU," she protested. Too late. The resident was already gone.

Leaving her little choice but to ignore her apprehension while helping to prepare a room for the new admission.

Luke pushed Mary Webster's bed through the hall himself, knowing that they didn't have a lot of time. The minute he hit the unit he gave orders. "Call the neonatal unit. I want a team up here with an isolette and all the necessary resuscitation equipment."

Caryn's eyes were wide but she hurried to do his bidding. Thank goodness the OB/GYN attending was there with him as to his knowledge there still wasn't a critical care intensivist around to cover him.

"I have a couple of our nurses bringing over some equipment as well," Dr. Gephart said, before using a Doppler to listen for fetal heart tones.

Luke's stomach clenched. "Do you anticipate taking Ms. Webster to the OR for a crash C-section?"

"No." Dr. Gephart shook his head. "If at all possible, I'd like to deliver her vaginally."

Luke didn't think it was possible for Caryn's eyes to grow any wider. "A vaginal delivery?" Her voice rose in a frightened squeak. *"Here?"*

"So far the fetus is doing fairly well, but I need you to bring down Mary Webster's blood pressure while maintaining her oxygenation saturations in the high nineties. And I want the critical care experts to take care of her once the baby has been delivered."

"I get that part, but *here*?" She didn't seem to realize

she was repeating herself. Caryn glanced around the already crowded bedside. "There isn't enough room to deliver a baby."

"We have to make room." Dr. Gephart obviously wasn't taking no for an answer. While he shared Caryn's trepidation, they didn't have time to waste arguing. He could have delivered the baby at a pinch but he was thankful he wouldn't have to this time.

"All right, Caryn, you and I are going to focus on taking care of the mother." Right now any structure was better than nothing and defining their roles helped to remind everyone they weren't doing anything they weren't trained for. He turned toward Dr. Gephart. "Delivering this baby is up to you and your nurses. This is not my area of expertise."

Dr. Gephart nodded and asked, "Where's the neonatal team?"

"On their way." Caryn's face was pale.

A couple of OB nurses entered the room, pushing a cart full of supplies. There was already a fetal heart monitor in place, and Luke was relieved to hear the reassuring yet rapid beat of the baby's heart. He dragged his attention to the matter at hand. His job was to care for the mother.

Don't think about Lisa. Don't.

"Caryn, let's draw another set of blood gases and I'd like to see Mary's systolic blood pressure maintained in the 160-170 range."

She nodded, drawing the blood from the patient's arterial line before he'd finished speaking. "I'm not familiar with the effects of magnesium sulfate. Can we add a vasodilator for her blood pressure?"

Dr. Gephart looked up from where he was arranging his equipment. "Yes, actually a vasodilator would be good for keeping the blood supply open for the baby, too."

"Go ahead and start some nitroglycerine," Luke told her.

She left the room with the blood gas specimen then returned a few minutes later with the bottle of nitro and tubing.

While she was hanging the medication, the neonatal team arrived, pushing a tall isolette and another tray of supplies. Since there wasn't enough space in the room, they placed the isolette just outside the door.

"All right, let's see if we can deliver this baby." Dr. Gephart didn't seem at all concerned about working in less than optimal conditions.

"The mother's blood pressure isn't responding to the nitro," Caryn said, worry evident in her tone. "She's still pretty high at 204 over 112."

Luke nodded, wondering if the pitocin that the OB nurse was infusing to cause contractions was also causing the patient's high blood pressure. "Increase her morphine, then. I want to make sure she's not awake through this."

Caryn increased the amount infusing from the IV pump, then swayed when the OB team propped up Mary Webster's legs, while doing their best to maintain her privacy. Luke grabbed her arm to keep her steady. Of all the nurses in the unit, it just figured she'd be the one forced to assist in this. If he thought he'd be able to convince Caryn to leave, he'd give it a try.

But one look at the thrust of her stubborn chin convinced him arguing was useless.

"She's still only seven centimeters dilated," Dr. Gephart observed. "We'll need to wait until she's reached ten centimeters."

Luke nodded, wondering for a moment where the expectant father was. Impending fatherhood had to be stressful enough without this added complication. Then again, it was possible the father wasn't involved.

He glanced for a moment at Caryn. If he was going to be a father, he'd insist on being a part of the baby's life. No matter what. As scary as fatherhood was, he'd never abandon his child the way his father had abandoned him.

One of the ICU nurses poked her head into the room, interrupting his thoughts. "Stat blood gas results for your patient on line one, Caryn."

Caryn pushed her way past the OB team, taking care not to gawk at the nearly crowning baby as she went to pick up the phone outside the room. In a few minutes she returned.

"Her PO2 is barely ninety," she said, handing Luke the results she'd hastily written on a scrap piece of paper. "And her PH is too high."

He didn't think trying to correct Mary Webster's alkalosis would work just yet, especially as the magnesium sulfate was probably the cause. But he planned to get everything ready for the moment she delivered.

"We'll keep an eye on it. I'm sure her magnesium level is high, too."

"Do you want me to send another set of electrolytes?" she asked. When he nodded she drew those, too, then once again left the room to send the blood sample to the lab. He watched Caryn walk away, wishing she'd had more than eight hours off after a twelve-hour shift.

He was also mad at himself for not waking up when she'd left.

She came back into the room in time to see Dr. Gephart pull out a large pair of forceps. The remaining color drained from her face.

"Stay with me, Caryn." Luke's sharp tone made her glance toward him and he held her gaze, willing her to focus on what needed to be done. "Come here, we have work to do."

For a moment she didn't move, then came around toward the head of the bed.

"Listen to the baby's heartbeat," he urged, as he changed the ventilator settings to provide more oxygen to mother and baby. Helping to keep Caryn calm was keeping his own anxiety under control. He could only be thankful he didn't have to participate in the actual delivery. "Don't dwell on what they're doing, let's just worry about the mother."

"All right." Her voice was faint but she picked up the clipboard and began writing down vital signs, although he'd be surprised if anyone would be able to decipher her handwriting the way her hands shook.

"She's at ten centimeters, so get ready." Dr. Gephart

had already draped the entire area in preparation for the birth. Luke was glad he and Caryn weren't able to see much from their location at the head of the bed.

"Here we go. There's the head. Now swipe the mucus away from the baby's mouth. There she is! Grab hold of her and clamp off the cord. Time of birth—0605."

The neonatal team surrounded the infant and once the umbilical cord was tied off and cut they whisked the baby to the isolette, providing necessary medical care.

"It's a girl." Dr. Gephart announced proudly as he prepared to receive the afterbirth.

Luke caught Caryn's gaze over the width of Mary Webster's bed.

Then he grinned, hearing the distinct sound of a baby's cry. Caryn smiled, too, her eyes suspiciously bright.

"The baby's fine, breathing on her own," Dr. Gephart said, bringing the newborn over.

Luke took the small bundle, looking down into the baby's wrinkled, crying face, and felt a sense of peace. As if by helping to save this tiny infant's life, he had eased some of the guilt he carried regarding his sister.

He raised his head and looked at Caryn. The hopeful expression on her face tugged at his heart. With a smile he handed the baby over to her and between them they arranged the mother's arms so they could place the infant next to her, regardless that Mary was still sedated.

As his fingers brushed Caryn's he realized how much he wanted to be there for her when it was her time to deliver.

And for her baby.

CHAPTER NINE

CARYN held onto the side rail of Mary's bed, gazing down at the tiny baby tucked in next to her mother. When Dr. Gephart had pulled out the most humungous forceps she'd ever seen, she'd wanted to shout "No" and throw herself in front of the mother, like a protester at a rally.

But Dr. Gephart obviously knew what he was doing, as Mary's baby was alive and fine. More than fine. Perfect. Beautiful. She glanced up at the monitor and noticed Mary's blood pressure had already dropped a few more points. Once the placenta had been delivered, Mary's blood pressure had begun dropping to a safer level. She was confident it would soon return to normal, as the treatment for eclampsia had simply been to deliver the baby.

Dr. Gephart finished with the episiotomy and stepped back. Keeping her gaze averted, Caryn stared at the monitor then jotted vital signs on the clipboard. There was no way she wanted to watch that part either. What on earth had she been thinking to get pregnant? She wasn't ready for this. To have a baby. To go through the process of giving birth.

She didn't need Debbie to act as a birthing coach—she needed a surrogate mother to have this baby for her.

Too bad she hadn't thought of that alternative *before* getting pregnant.

Her blanched face drew Luke's attention. "Don't worry. This is an extreme case. The chances are slim anything like this would happen to you." Luke's tone held a false sense of cheerfulness she wasn't buying. "You'll be fine."

She bit back a tart response. Luke stared at her as if he wanted to say more, but he didn't.

Just as Dr. Gephart finished cleaning up the area, a man came running down the hall. "Is she here? Mary? Is my wife here?"

She exchanged a surprised glance with Luke then stepped back to allow the breathless man to come up to the bedside.

"Mr. Webster? I'm Dr. Hamilton. Your wife is still sedated but your daughter is fine."

Mr. Webster stared down at his tiny daughter, then back to his wife, who was still breathing with the help of the ventilator. Caryn's heart squeezed when his eyes widened in alarm. "Dear God. Will she be all right? Will she wake up? Breathe on her own?"

"Yes, we had to put the breathing tube in because she was having seizures, but she's all right now," Luke assured him. "As soon as all her vitals return to normal and she wakes up, we'll be able to take the breathing tube out."

"Thank God." Mary's husband closed his eyes for a minute then leaned over to kiss his wife and his newborn daughter. His voice was low, husky. "If we had a girl, Mary wanted to name her Lindsey, after her mother."

Caryn smiled, the obvious love in his eyes bringing her close to tears. "Lindsey is a beautiful name."

He reached for the baby, then hesitated and glanced at Caryn as if to seek permission. "Is it all right if I hold her?"

"Of course." She lifted Lindsey from where they'd tucked the baby next to her mother and handed the bundle over. Mary's husband stared down at his daughter with a look of awe.

Suddenly Caryn was ashamed at how she'd feared the process of giving birth. The miracle of creating a tiny life was worth every ounce of discomfort. The devoted love shining in the new father's eyes filled her with a mixture of hope and envy.

She caught Luke staring at her from across the room and wondered what it would be like to have his strength and support when her time came.

But then she looked away, knowing deep down she was greedy. Because she'd didn't just want Luke's strength as a friend. Friends were important, but she wanted more.

She wanted love, like Mary Webster had from her husband.

She wanted it all.

"We'll send an OB nurse over each shift to check on Mom," Sally, the OB nurse, promised, once all the excitement had died down. "And, of course, Dr. Gephart and his team will keep an eye on her, too."

"Will someone bring the baby back when she wakes up?" Caryn asked.

"Give us a call when the medication wears off and we'll arrange a visit," Sally assured her.

Once everyone had left, Caryn tried to concentrate on what she needed to do next. Routine ICU care seemed a bit anticlimactic compared to the excitement of delivering a baby.

"Are you sure you're all right?" Luke asked, coming up behind her.

"Yes." She was hyper-aware of his presence, remembering those stolen moments in his call room. She'd never felt as safe as she had in Luke's arms. "I need to thank you," she said in a low voice. "Your calm attitude kept me from freaking out during Mary's delivery."

He shook his head. "You don't have to thank me. Believe me, I understood how you felt. For a few minutes there I wasn't doing too well myself."

Luke was being awfully nice about this. Especially since she knew very well she wouldn't have made it through without him. "You were great. I can only hope and pray that my delivery goes without any complications."

"It will." He frowned. "Although, now that I think about it, maybe we need to hire you a birthing coach. Someone who's an expert in the field."

Her brows shot up at his suggestion. "No, I don't think that's necessary." There was no way she could afford something like that. "I trust my doctor. She's the expert, right?

"I just don't think you should go through this alone," he said in a serious tone.

It was on the tip of her tongue to suggest he take the role, until she realized how pushy that sounded. A few kisses didn't mean anything. Heck, she didn't think Luke was in the market for a ready-made family. She cleared her throat. "Ah, David's sister Debbie volunteered to be my birthing coach. Don't worry, I won't be alone."

There was a long pause as Luke stared at her, as if he might offer to take over for Debbie. But he didn't. He simply nodded and stepped back. "Good. That's good." Luke glanced down when his pager went off. "Blasted thing," he muttered. "Sorry, I have to go, but I'll talk to you later."

"Sure." She fell silent as he hurried away, trying to stifle an acute stab of disappointment. Luke wasn't obligated to do anything he didn't want to. She didn't have a right to depend on him.

She squared her shoulders. She'd be much better off to remain independent and self-supporting.

If only that didn't sound so lonely.

"Dr. Hamilton? I think you'd better come and look at this guy in room twelve. He just came back from Radiology where they placed a right subclavian central line and the right side of his face and chest is puffy."

Luke crossed over to the bedside. His pulse skipped several beats when he saw the patient, Mr. Albert, with his face swollen like a balloon.

"Get me the largest needle you can find," Luke ordered. "Hurry!"

"What's going on?" Caryn entered the room.

The nurse, Anna, was haphazardly digging through the supply cabinet. "He needs a needle."

"Use this fourteen-gauge." Caryn plucked it from the pile and handed it to him, along with a syringe.

"Thanks." He took a deep breath, then counted Mr. Albert's ribs as best as he could with the air trapped underneath and then quickly inserted the needle between the fourth and fifth intercostal space. The man flinched and a loud hissing sound filled the room.

"It worked." Caryn glanced up at the monitor over Mr. Albert's bed. "Did anyone check if he has a pulse with that heart rhythm?"

"I didn't think of that," Anna said in a sheepish tone. "I just couldn't believe how his face was growing puffy, swelling up right before my eyes."

Luke put his fingers on the patient's carotid artery, waiting until he felt the reassuring beat of his pulse, then nodded. "Thankfully, he has a pulse now, but you'd better check his blood pressure."

"Still a bit on the low side, at 88 over 56." Anna glanced at him. "He doesn't have another line, so we can't start any vasopressors until he has a new line placed."

Luke clenched his jaw at the latest problem but remained calm. "First I need to put a larger chest tube in. Can you find me a chest tube insertion tray?"

"Yes, I'll get it." Caryn left the room.

His stomach cramped but he did his best to ignore it

as he grabbed some antiseptic solution from the cart and began to prep the skin of Mr. Albert's chest around the fourteen-gauge needle. A bead of sweat slid down the center of his back and he suspected he was running a fever. Hopefully no one would notice.

"I have the tray." Caryn set it on a nearby table and began to unwrap the sterile drapes around the tray, while keeping the contents sterile.

"Thanks." He pulled on a cap, mask, sterile gown and sterile gloves then reached for the sterile drapes in the tray. He carefully placed them around the planned insertion site and then reached for the needle and syringe pre-filled with lidocaine so he could numb the skin. Once he'd accomplished that, he picked up the scalpel and hesitated. There was a fine tremor in his hand, and he wanted to think it was from the fever rather than nerves.

Taking a deep breath, as much as he could through his sterile mask, he used the scalpel to incise a small area right below the needle. Sweat dampened his forehead beneath the surgical cap.

"Are you all right?" Caryn frowned. "You look flushed, as if you're running a fever."

"I'm fine." He concentrated on making a one-inch opening then used the trochanter to insert the large chest tube between the ribs. Ever since the on-call resident had gotten him out of bed to help with Mrs. Webster's delivery, his stomach had been getting progressively worse. But he didn't have time to be sick so he did his best to ignore the cramping pain. Once he had the chest tube in place, he glanced at Caryn. "Do you have a water-seal hook-up for me?"

"Right here." Caryn hung the chest-tube container from the end of the bed, then held out the end he'd need to connect to the chest tube.

"Why did Radiology put this line in?" he asked as he made the connection and then grabbed a suture to secure the chest tube so it wouldn't become dislodged.

"We didn't know how long you were going to be tied up in the delivery and his other line clotted off," Anna responded from her position on the other side of the bed. "He needed antibiotics so the resident decided to call Radiology for help." Anna flashed him a chagrined look. "Was that wrong?"

"No, it wasn't wrong." They didn't routinely send their patients to Radiology for line placements, but there had been nothing normal about the circumstances over the past twenty-four hours. He honestly couldn't blame the resident for making the best decision he could at the time. Better to send the patient to Radiology than to try to put the line in himself without proper supervision.

If he went home sick, the residents would have no supervision.

"You really don't look very good." Caryn's brow was pulled together in a frown.

He avoided her gaze, suspecting she'd be able to tell he was lying. "Too much adrenaline from the delivery." He finished with the chest tube then stripped off his gown and mask. "Now he needs another central line."

"Why don't you have one of the residents do it?" Caryn said in a low tone. "You can supervise."

She was absolutely right, he thought in relief. "Good idea. Help him set up for the procedure, would you? I'll be right back."

He left the unit at what he thought was an unhurried walk, considering how badly he wanted to run. But when he returned from the bathroom, Caryn met him outside Mr. Albert's room.

"Hold it." She grabbed his arm. It was a sign how weak he felt when he wanted to gather her close and lean on her for support. "Look at me."

Doing as she'd asked, he steeled himself to meet her gaze.

She sucked in a swift breath, seeing right through him to the truth. "Oh, no. You're sick with *Crypto,* too, aren't you?"

"Stay away from me," Luke warned, trying to shake her hand off. Despite his best efforts, she only tightened her grip. Stubborn woman. "I'm contagious. I don't want you to get sick, too."

"You need to call someone in to cover you." She frowned. "Actually, now that I think about it, where in the heck is Mitch? I'm surprised he's not here with everything that's been going on."

"He's sick, too." Luke swiped his forehead with the back of his arm. "There isn't anyone else to cover. Mitch was making phone calls yesterday but everyone he called was also sick."

Her eyes widened. "I had no idea things were so bad."

They weren't that bad. Yet.

"Let me grab that chair over there for you." Before he could stop her, she darted away then returned, dragging a chair.

"Thanks, but I won't be able to watch the procedure if I sit." The patient lying in the bed was at a much higher level than the seat of the chair.

She scoffed. "He's not even close to the part you need to watch. Sit down." She pushed him into the chair and he sat. Or maybe his knees buckled. "I'll gown up and make sure he doesn't contaminate anything. When we get to the part where he needs to cannulate the vein, I'll let you know so you can watch."

Luke wished he didn't feel as weak as Mary Webster's baby as he leaned back in the chair. As soon as this line was placed and Mr. Albert's care was under control, he'd go back to see how Mary was doing.

Another cramp hit him and he realized he couldn't keep ignoring his illness. Antibiotics weren't normally needed for healthy patients with *Crypto* but as he was there alone, he thought maybe his case would be an exception. If he took several doses of antibiotics, he might be able to continue working. Struggling to his feet, he crossed to the nearest phone, keeping his voice down as he requested medication from the pharmacy. The pharmacist didn't argue.

"I'll send some up, but we're running low on supplies. We're expecting a special shipment later today, though."

That's right, today was Sunday. The days were blurring together as if they were one continuous never-ending shift. He glanced at his watch—it was almost eight o'clock in the morning. "I can wait for the new shipment if you need the medication for our hospital-ized patients. What time are you expecting it to arrive?"

"Not until noon." The pharmacist sounded apologetic. "There's a huge demand for the stuff throughout the city."

Yeah, no joke. He swallowed hard, not sure he'd be able to wait until noon. "Are you sure you have enough to spare?"

"Yes, we should have enough."

The pharmacist didn't exactly sound sure, but he wasn't going to keep arguing. "I'll take it, then, thanks."

He waited for the medication to arrive via the pneu-matic tube system then gulped it down with filtered water. When he returned to Mr. Albert's room, Caryn and the resident were ready for him.

"All right, show me your landmarks." He talked the resident through the procedure and thankfully this time the line went in without difficulty.

"Get a chest X-ray to verify placement," Luke ordered. "And clean up the mess, especially making sure you find every one of your sharps. The nurses have more important things to do than to clean up after you."

Caryn shot him a surprised look then covered a quick grin. He stared at her, remembering how beautiful she'd looked, like Sleeping Beauty, in his arms. Despite feeling like he'd been leveled by an eighteen-wheeler, his body tightened at the mere thought of holding her again.

His smile faded. He hoped to heaven he hadn't

exposed her to *Crypto* during their brief time together in his call room. Because if he had, he'd never forgive himself for making her sick.

And potentially risking her unborn baby.

Caryn was exhausted by the time her second twelve-hour shift was over. Never in her whole life had she worked so hard for so long.

The entire unit had handled one crisis after another until they'd finally gotten things under control.

She glanced around the unit, looking for Luke, wondering where he'd gone. She hadn't seen him for the past couple of hours, although she knew the poor guy had been making frequent trips to the bathroom.

"Anna, have you seen Dr. Hamilton lately?" she asked.

"Not since one of the residents took him down to the ED," Anna said in a vague tone.

What? "He was taken to the ED? You mean like a patient?" How had she missed that?

"Yeah. I'm sure he'll be fine after a couple of liters of fluid." Anna shrugged and walked off.

Caryn left the unit and took the elevator straight down to the emergency department. The place looked as chaotic as the ICU had been. She waylaid one of the ED nurses before she could rush past. "Do you still have Dr. Luke Hamilton down here?"

"No, we gave him two liters of IV fluids then discharged him."

"Thanks for letting me know." Caryn turned and left, wondering where Luke had gone. She headed down to her assigned call room, her steps slowing as she passed his door.

Shouldn't someone make sure he's all right? She lifted her hand and knocked. "Luke?" she called in a low tone. "Are you in there?"

Putting her ear to the door, she listened but didn't hear any response. She tried the doorhandle but the door was locked.

Was he even in there? Or had the ED sent him home? She knocked again, but after waiting a few minutes without a response made her way down the hall to her own room.

Maybe he had been sent home. Being sick with *Crypto* was no picnic. No doubt he felt awful. She couldn't blame him for wanting nothing more than to go home.

Silly to be disappointed that he hadn't found her to say goodbye.

CHAPTER TEN

CARYN was glad that early on Monday afternoon the hospital administration at Trinity Medical Center declared the *Cryptosporidium* emergency officially over. Nursing staff infected with the bug were already bouncing back from the city-wide epidemic, and the hospital had gone from a record high of 248 sick calls over three days down to 31.

The staff nurses who'd been at the hospital during the emergency were allowed to go home, although they were all asked to be on call should the need arise. Luckily, many nurses had responded to the crisis and those who lived outside Milwaukee had come in to lighten the burden on the remaining staff.

Caryn left the hospital without having seen Luke since the day before. An attending physician, Dr. Billar, had shown up to replace Mitch, quickly taking control of the residents in the unit. Twice Caryn had picked up the phone to page Luke, but had then set the phone back down, figuring he wouldn't have his pager turned on if he was sick. She didn't know his home phone number and was too embarrassed to ask.

Since he hadn't made a point of talking to her before he'd left, she figured he didn't want her interfering anyway. That fact didn't stop her from imagining Luke lying at home in bed too sick to move. Was he able to eat? Keep fluids down?

She hoped so.

The only good thing about being stuck at the hospital during the *Crypto* crisis was that she'd be paid for the entire time she'd been there, even the time she'd technically been off duty. The overtime she'd racked up would come in very handy in paying off the second mortgage David had spent.

The sun was shining and the temperature was warming up nicely when she drove home. Spring had finally hit Milwaukee and she liked seeing the tiny buds opening up on the trees. The delicate scent of apple blossom was in the air and she took a deep breath then sneezed when pollen tickled her nose.

She walked into her small house, feeling as if she'd been gone for weeks instead of a few days. Everything was just as she'd left it, including the half-open bags of hand-me-down maternity clothes courtesy of Debbie and Renee.

Idly, she wondered how David was doing. No doubt Debbie expected her to show up at the neuro-rehab center to see him, but she just couldn't do it. The reminder of David's family made her sink into her sofa, burying her face in her hands.

How long? How much longer would she have to

pretend to feel something she didn't? How long before she could tell David's family the truth?

David had been seriously injured and, no matter how strained their relationship had been, she surely owed the father of her child something? She'd been far more worried about Luke, who could take care of himself, or at the very least pick up a phone to call for help. David couldn't do anything.

She should visit, if only for the sake of his family. And she would. But not yet. After being at work for over forty-eight hours straight, she deserved a little down time. At least she'd been granted three consecutive days off from work, despite being placed on call, which would give her plenty of time to relax.

To face David's family.

To gather enough strength to keep from blurting the truth.

To think about Luke and wonder if they really teetered on the verge of a relationship or if her over-active imagination had caused her to see something that wasn't there?

On Wednesday Dana dragged Caryn out shopping. Even though she couldn't afford to spend any money, Caryn didn't mind tagging along. People-watching at the mall was always fun.

"Be thankful you didn't get *Crypto*," Dana said as they walked into the Grand Avenue Mall located in downtown Milwaukee. "I can't believe how sick Mitch and I were."

"Has Mitch heard from Luke?" Caryn asked, keeping her tone casual. "I know he was sick, too."

"Yeah, he's feeling better." Dana frowned as they stopped at a dress shop. "I have to find a dress for this weekend. Mitch wants me to go with him to a fundraiser sponsored by Trinity Medical Center."

"So what's wrong with that?" Caryn asked, trying not to be depressed while eyeing dresses she wouldn't fit into for a long time. "Sounds like fun."

Dana wrinkled her nose. "They're not really. Too much mingling and chatting."

Caryn pulled out a black dress slit down to the navel. "Bet Mitch would like this one," she teased.

Dana rolled her eyes. "Oh, please, don't give him any ideas."

Grinning, she put it back on the rack. A few minutes later another woman entered the store and picked up the same risqué dress, going straight to the dressing room to try it on.

Caryn looked at Dana and they both burst out laughing.

"I have to say, Caryn, you seem so much happier without David."

She glanced at Dana in surprise. "Really?"

Dana nodded. "I never liked him much," she confided. "You were too good for him."

Knowing that her friends had sensed her misery made her sigh. She should have confided in them a long time ago. "David had…a lot of problems." The middle of a dress shop wasn't the place to go into detail.

"I suspected as much. But it doesn't matter now.

You're better off without him." Dana held a royal blue dress in front of her. "What do you think?"

"I like it. Try it on," she urged.

Dana added it to a growing pile slung over her arm.

A maternity store across the way caught Caryn's eye and as it seemed Dana would be a while, she murmured, "I'll be right back."

Drawn by the display in the window, she left Dana with her armful of dresses and crossed over to the small store. She felt silly even looking, considering she didn't need clothes. Debbie and Renee had given her more than enough things to wear.

Except the clothes in the store were beautiful, flattering in a way that emphasized a woman's pregnancy, celebrating it. For a moment she remembered Luke telling her she was a total turn-on and she blushed, thinking that she'd feel sexy in some of these items, which were far more stylish than the older clothes that had been donated to her.

The prices were outrageous, though, too high for her tight budget, so she turned away. No matter how tempting, she couldn't waste money on things she didn't need. Especially when there would be more than enough baby items to buy.

She made her way through the mall crowds and, to her surprise, ran straight into Luke.

"Caryn!" He greeted her with a smile. He had a garment bag draped over his shoulder. His gaze swung from the maternity store to her empty hands. "Didn't find what you were looking for?"

"I'm just window-shopping." She waved a hand casually, shying away from the bare truth. Not that it really mattered, as he knew more about her strained financial situation than most of her friends did. Luke looked better, healthier than the last time she'd seen him. Her gaze sought his. "How are you feeling? I heard from Anna you had to go down to the ED for IV fluids."

"Yeah, but I'm fine now." He glanced at the floor, as if embarrassed to have succumbed to something so mundane as illness. His brows came together in a frown and his eyes held concern. "How about you? I hope I didn't cause you to get sick, too?"

"Nope, I'm healthy as can be." Was that the reason he hadn't come to see her when he'd left? Because he'd been worried she might become contaminated with *Crypto,* too? The tightness around her heart eased a little. David had been very self-centered. This was the second time Luke had put her needs ahead of his own.

"Thank heavens," Luke said in a heartfelt tone. "Are you here alone?" He glanced around. "We could have lunch."

She wanted nothing more than to eat lunch with Luke, but that wouldn't be fair to Dana so she shook her head with very real regret. "As much as I'd like to, I'm not alone. I'm here with Dana. She's waiting for me."

"I see." He looked a little disappointed.

"Maybe another time?" she asked hopefully.

"Sure. Take care, Caryn." He flashed that lethal smile of his again and stepped back, giving her room to move past him.

"I will. Bye, Luke." She headed toward the dress shop where she'd left Dana, resisting the urge to glance back at him over her shoulder. Before she could enter the dress shop, a toddler threw herself on the floor of the mall, screaming at the top of her lungs in the best display of a temper tantrum Caryn had ever seen.

Mall customers stopped and stared. A young couple standing next to a stroller argued for a few minutes about the best way to handle their daughter. Finally the child's father picked up the girl, mindless of her kicking and screaming, and headed straight to the mall exit, while the young mother followed with the stroller.

Good choice, Caryn thought, but then her smile faded. At least the parents had each other to talk to about these sorts of things. When she'd first realized she was pregnant she'd made the decision to raise her child alone, accepting the responsibility. But since she'd begun to spend more time with Luke she'd found her conviction to remain independent wavering.

Was she exaggerating her attraction to Luke as a way to subconsciously avoid being a single parent?

A tiny knot formed in her stomach, giving an uneasy twist. She'd met David shortly after her parents had died and at the time he'd seemed so kind and gentle. She'd thought herself in love with him and had asked him to move in with her, only to later realize she'd made a huge mistake.

Now here she was on the brink of getting involved with Luke during another crisis in her life. How could she trust she wouldn't make the same mistake again?

* * *

Luke entered the maternity store and immediately noticed he was the only guy in the place. Women openly gawked at him. He scowled. For Pete's sake, didn't men buy maternity clothes for their wives? With a resigned shrug he looked around, trying to figure out which outfit had caught Caryn's eye.

The clothes she had on were once again too large for her small frame, not to mention they were clearly hand-me-downs. She deserved something new, something special. He gazed at a pink top with a beaded diamond in the center on a pregnant mannequin, and easily imagined Caryn wearing it instead.

Taking the top from the rack, he added two pairs of leggings, knowing they'd show off Caryn's shapely legs. Although she'd look great no matter what she wore. Then he spied a black clingy dress that would look perfect on her and grabbed that, too.

He didn't normally spend a lot of time in shopping malls, but he'd needed to purchase a new tux for a charity event Mitch had asked him to attend. Apparently the hospital was also using the event to thank everyone who'd worked so hard during the *Crypto* crisis. When he'd seen Caryn coming out of the maternity store, he was so glad to see her he'd walked straight toward her without thinking twice about what he'd been doing.

Her concern over his well-being was heartwarming, although he told himself not to read too much into her comments. Caryn cared about everyone, especially her patients. He'd been glad to hear he hadn't caused her to get sick. He'd had no business encouraging her to spend the night with him in his call room, no matter how much he'd enjoyed kissing her, touching her and eventually sleeping with her in his arms. Although those moments had sustained him during his illness, he'd dreamed of her often, waking up tense and hot and sweaty, and not from a fever.

He paid for the maternity clothes he'd picked out for Caryn, knowing buying personal items for her was crossing the line yet unable to stop himself. He alternated between his desperate need to see her and the agonizing fear of caring too much. He didn't know anything about relationships. His father had left before he'd been old enough to go to school and his mother had gone through men quicker than most people drank rare wine.

Was he really ready to jump into a relationship?

His stomach clenched. As much as he was very attracted to Caryn, he didn't really know anything about being a husband or a father. What if things didn't work out? It wouldn't be easy to walk away.

Not when one considered there was the added responsibility of a child that needed to be taken into consideration, too.

He tossed the maternity clothes and his new tux in the back seat of his car and told himself he was getting way ahead of things. He and Caryn had shared a few stolen moments but they hadn't even gone out on a proper date.

Although that could change, if he invited her to attend the charity ball with him.

Would she agree? Or turn him down flat?

There was only one way to know for sure.

That evening, Luke finagled Caryn's address from Mitch and drove over to her house. The clothes he'd bought for her were in brightly colored gift-wrapped boxes on the seat beside him.

He debated how best to present them to her. No matter how he tried to frame it, the clothes were a very personal gift. He could leave them for her anonymously, but then he wouldn't have the added benefit of spending time with her.

He pulled up in front of her house and sat for a minute.

Surveying her home, he was not surprised to find the house was well maintained. There was a small but cozy yard just big enough for a swing set. He could easily imagine Caryn pushing her small daughter on the swing, then gave himself a mental shake. Caryn's baby wouldn't need a swing set for years yet.

And he'd stalled long enough.

Picking up the boxes, he climbed from the car and headed up to the front door. The inside front door was open, and his fingers tightened on the gifts when he realized she was actually home. He pressed on the doorbell, listening as it echoed through the house.

"Coming!" she called, from somewhere in the back. Through the screen door he saw her come around the corner, a paintbrush in one hand and a smear of yellow paint across her cheek.

Her steps slowed, her eyes widening in surprise when she saw him standing there. "Luke. What are you doing here?"

"Hi, Caryn." He wondered what she was painting then reminded himself it was none of his business. "I was in the neighborhood and thought I'd stop by." *Lame, Hamilton,* he thought. *Really lame.*

"Come in." She opened the door and stepped back, inviting him in.

"I don't mean to barge in on you, but here." He held out the gifts. "This is for you."

She didn't take the boxes but clutched the yellow-tipped paintbrush like a torch, so she wouldn't smear more paint on her T-shirt and sweatpants stretched over her belly. A frown tugged at the corners of her mouth. "Luke, you're not supposed to buy me gifts."

"I know, but I wanted to." An awkward silence fell and he mentally cursed himself for not simply leaving the boxes outside her door. When she made no move to take the gifts, he glanced around her tidy living room. "Nice place. What are you painting?"

"Thanks."

When she didn't say anything more, he set the boxes down. "I'll just leave these here, then. You can open them later."

She narrowed her gaze as if tempted to call his bluff. Then, with obvious reluctance, she took the boxes. Crossing over to the sofa, she sat down, cradling the gifts on her lap. She set the paintbrush on the edge of the table, bristles outward to keep from getting paint on her furniture.

He stood, watching her. When she opened the first box and lifted the tissue paper, she gasped. "Luke, it's beautiful."

She carefully lifted the shell-pink maternity top from the box and held it up against herself, touching the tiny pink pearls stitched into the silky soft fabric.

"I'm glad you like it." There were more boxes to open, but she wasn't looking at the gifts, only at him.

"How did you know my size?" She asked with suspicion.

"A lucky guess." He shoved his hands in his pockets to keep from reaching for her. "I wanted you to have some of your own maternity clothes, not just hand-me-downs."

Her eyes widened and she looked at the boxes. "Some? How much more?"

"Just a few things." He couldn't wait to see her wearing them. Especially the dress.

She opened a second box and held up the black dress. "Ah—where in the world did you think I'm going to wear this?"

He cleared his throat. "There's a charity ball this weekend that I need to attend. Maybe you'd be willing to go with me? The hospital is planning to give a big thank-you to those of us who worked during the *Crypto* crisis."

She stared at him, then abruptly folded the dress and placed it back in its box. "Luke, why did you do this?" She looked distressed as she set the box aside and twisted her hands together. "Did I somehow give you the impression that I wanted you to buy me these clothes this afternoon?"

He frowned. "No. Of course not."

She continued as if she wasn't listening. "Because if so, I'm sorry. That honestly wasn't my intention. I shouldn't have even gone into the stupid store. I don't need brand-new maternity clothes. Debbie's hand-me-downs will work just fine."

He crossed over toward her. "Caryn, stop it. You didn't hint that I should buy anything. This was my own idea, I swear."

"I don't think I should accept these gifts, Luke." She stood, grabbed her paintbrush from the table and headed down the hall.

He followed as she turned into a small, empty bedroom with old sheets spread out to protect the floor. A bucket of yellow paint sat in the middle of the floor and a ladder, with a paint tray and roller, stood by the farthest wall.

"Caryn, what are you doing?" He frowned when she headed straight for the ladder.

"I'm painting my nursery." There was a stubborn slant to her chin as she placed her foot on the bottom rung then took another step. "Don't try to tell me what to do."

He was hardly listening. "Get off that ladder, for crying out loud. What if you fall?"

She narrowed her gaze. "I'm not going to fall. In the
ook you gave me it mentions how most falls are a

result of being off balance, and I'm not big enough to have that problem."

"Get down." He rolled up the sleeves of his shirt. "You're not doing this. Step aside, I'll paint for you."

"No, you won't. This is my nursery. I don't need you telling me what to do. Go home, Luke. Stop being such a bully."

Her accusation hit hard. "I'm sorry." He lowered his tone, trying not to raise his voice. He stepped closer to the ladder, wishing he could lift her off to get her feet on solid ground. "I'm just worried about you, Caryn."

"Don't. I'm not a charity case. I don't need you to buy me pretty clothes. I don't need you to paint my nursery. I'm perfectly capable of raising this baby on my own."

CHAPTER ELEVEN

CARYN knew she'd overreacted the moment Luke closed the door behind him as he left.

But she didn't call him back.

Mortification still clogged the back of her throat when she thought about the gifts he'd brought her. Then he'd asked her to go to the ball and she hadn't known what to say. Was she ready to take this next step in their relationship? What if she was mixing up her feelings for Luke with the fear of being alone?

So she'd avoided giving him an answer. Then he'd yelled at her and she'd yelled back, calling him a bully. Logically, she knew Luke wasn't David, but when he'd come across so strong, ordering her to get down, her knee-jerk response had been automatic. When David had moved in with her, he'd taken over almost every aspect of her life, running things the way he'd wanted.

She believed Luke did care about her. But she really wasn't a charity case, no matter how Luke obviously ought otherwise. A helping hand was one thing, but basically coming into her house and taking over was something else entirely.

And where would she draw the line? What was next? Paying off her second mortgage?

No. She really was capable of standing on her own two feet. Calmer now, she finished painting the wall, then cleaned up the mess and put everything away. When she returned to the living room, she noticed Luke's gift boxes still sitting in the middle of her coffee-table.

Against her better judgment she picked up the pink maternity top and held it against herself. The shimmery blouse matched her coloring perfectly. The urge to try on the new clothes was overwhelming.

But she couldn't keep them. Dropping the top back inside its box, she turned away.

She needed to make Luke understand that she wasn't some damsel in distress that he needed to rescue.

Instead, she'd rather be the woman he was attracted to.

Caryn returned to work on Friday, but her path didn't cross Luke's. Her patients were stable and the residents assigned to take care of them were capable enough, answering her questions and writing the orders she needed.

A part of her longed to see Luke again but another part of her knew he'd expect an answer to his invitation. If the offer was even still open. For all she knew, he'd invited someone else.

"Hi, Caryn." Michelle found her just before lunch. "I have something for you." She handed Caryn an envelope.

"What is it?" Caryn asked with a frown.

"An invitation to the charity ball on Saturday night. There's a special thank-you for all the staff members who helped out during the *Crypto* emergency."

"Oh, I've heard about that. Thanks, Michelle." Caryn tucked the invitation into her purse. She could easily imagine wearing the dress Luke had bought her, even though she knew she couldn't keep it. "I'll have to think about going."

"Please, do. You deserve some fun after the long shifts you put in here," Michelle urged. "I'm going, I have a babysitter to watch Brianna."

"Great." Caryn's smile faded as she walked away. Was she brave enough to go alone? Why not? If she was really going to do this single-parent thing she had better get used to doing things on her own.

Luke would be there, of course, but she couldn't expect to avoid him for ever. The typical critical care fellowship program was for three years and she wasn't leaving a job she loved because of him.

Caryn had to work again on Saturday, but she was off on Sunday, which was a good thing because if she decided to go to the ball, she wouldn't have to be up early the next day.

Later that evening, she did a load of laundry and walked past the gift boxes she'd never gotten around to returning to Luke. The boxes seemed to draw her gaze every time she went past until finally she stopped and opened one.

Giving in to temptation, she drew out the black dress, took it into her bedroom and put it on. The silky fabric draped her figure, clinging to her plump breasts in a way that emphasized her curves. She didn't want to buy maternity stockings, so she tried a pair of thigh-highs with modest heels, and then critically surveyed her reflection in the mirror from all sides.

If not for the modest bulge of her stomach, she didn't really look all that pregnant, she decided. And Luke's dress flattered her figure far more than the boxy dress of Debbie's she'd tried on the previous day.

Turning away from the mirror, she sighed. Who was she kidding? She wanted to keep the dress. Maybe she could just pay him back. Because no matter how much she tried to tell herself otherwise, she knew darned well she wanted to look nice, attractive, and sexy.

For Luke.

Caryn's stomach fluttered with nerves as she parked her car and mounted the steps leading to the hotel. This was one of the oldest, most elegant hotels in Milwaukee, the place where all the famous people stayed while they were in town. She'd known about the hotel for years but had never once been inside the grand ballroom.

Until now.

Elegant chandeliers sparkled brightly overhead and shimmery fabric draped the walls. A band played background music as people milled around, tasting various hors d'oeuvres, until it was time for dinner. Rumor had it there would be after-dinner dancing as well. Caryn noticed there were many physicians and upper-management types in attendance, but not quite as many nurses. She ran into Dana and Mitch just as they were about to sit down for dinner. She eagerly joined them, relieved to sit with someone she knew.

Luke snuck into the empty seat beside her before she could blink. "Hi, Caryn," he greeted her in a low, husky tone. "You look beautiful tonight."

"Thanks." She flushed and could have kicked herself for her instant physical awareness of him, but, darn it, he'd caught her off guard. The mere sight of him stole her breath. Luke in a tux should be declared illegal. A sensual danger to women everywhere. She was suddenly very glad she'd worn the silky dress.

Luckily, Mitch quickly engaged Luke in conversation, leaving her to concentrate on eating her meal without spilling a good portion of her salad greens topped with a light raspberry vinaigrette dressing into her lap. When Luke leaned toward her a few minutes later, she caught a whiff of his spicy aftershave and thought he smelt better than anything on her plate.

"Thank you for keeping the dress," he murmured. "It suits you perfectly."

She fingered the fabric of her dress, knowing deep down he was right. "You have very good taste."

His lips quirked in a smile. "For once we agree."

Caryn gulped her water, glad she wasn't able to have anything stronger, considering Luke's attentiveness was enough to drive her senses haywire. She had no idea what she ate for the main course of their meal, but it must have been good.

The after-dinner program was short, but after the CEO of the hospital gave his heartfelt thanks to all the staff who had pulled together during the *Crypto* crisis, there was a standing ovation. Luke winked and caught her hand in his and she ducked her head, knowing he was remembering the lingering kisses and the night they'd shared in his call room.

The CEO had no idea that working through the *Crypto* crisis hadn't been all bad.

As the banquet staff cleared tables off the dance floor, Caryn debated slipping away. Not because she was afraid to dance, but did she really want to be a third wheel to Dana and Mitch if Luke decided he needed to mingle and talk to other guests?

"Where are you going?" Luke asked when she stood.

"I, uh, thought I'd better get home."

"Already?" Luke quickly rose to his feet. "Are you really too tired? Won't you stay, at least for a little while longer?"

"Ah…sure. Why not?" She honestly didn't put up much of an argument as she wanted to stay more than anything. When the band began to play, she glanced over at the dance floor, noticing many couples already heading there.

"Dance with me?" Luke asked, taking her hand once again in his.

She nodded and allowed him to lead her onto the dance floor, feeling like a modern-day Cinderella. Luke pulled her into his arms, his arms strong and warm around her. She expected her rounded stomach to get in the way, but their bodies fit together perfectly as if she weren't pregnant at all.

"I'm glad you changed your mind about coming tonight," Luke murmured. "And about the other day, I'm sorry. I never meant to be a bully."

Ashamed at how she'd overreacted, she shook her head. "You weren't, not really. I'm the one who's sorry. I shouldn't have said that."

"No, you were right. I was trying to tell you what to do. Being bossy comes naturally to physicians." He held her gaze with his. "Forgive me?"

How could she not? "Of course."

He bent his head and kissed her, just the lightest brush of his mouth on hers, but the way his arms tightened around her she realized he was holding himself in check in deference to being surrounded by people they both worked with.

He lifted his head and slid a hand down into the small of her back, urging her closer. Heat pooled in her groin as they brushed against each other, swaying to the beat of the music.

She realized the song had ended when he slowed to a stop. "Caryn?"

"Hmm?" she tipped her head back to see him.

"Will you let me take you home?"

She sucked in a breath, knowing this was about more than just simply offering her a lift, but the knowledge of what she was really getting into didn't stop her from nodding. "Yes."

"Great." The relief on his face was almost comical. He grabbed her hand. "Let's go."

She wanted to laugh at his eagerness, but the anticipation flickering through her veins understood his barely repressed urgency. "Wait." She tried to marshal her thoughts. "I should probably let Dana and Mitch know." She glanced around for the couple as Luke led the way back toward their table. "Where did they go? They were just here."

"I see them. Sit here for a minute and rest your feet. I'll tell them we're leaving." Luke threaded his way through the crowd.

She sat and clutched her evening bag with tight fingers. She forced herself to relax. During this whole evening Luke had treated her as a woman, as someone he was attracted to instead of someone he worried about.

This was exactly what she'd wanted.

Watching him saying something to Dana and Mitch, she smiled, tempted to kick off her heels but more worried that if she did, she'd never get them back on. She moved from side to side, trying to stretch her back muscles, which lately had been tightening with spasms for no reason.

Finally the impatient waiting was over. Luke returned and offered his arm. "Ready?"

"Sure." She took his arm but as they made their way to the front entrance a tiny kernel of doubt crept in. The valet service would fetch his car, but then hers would be stuck there. She didn't want to be left at home, dependent on Luke for a ride. "Maybe I should just drive my own car home," she murmured. "Then I don't have to figure out how to get my car back."

"How about we take your car home instead?" Luke

suggested. "I'll leave my car here. I can get one of the residents to give me a lift later."

Once more she was surprised at his thoughtfulness. Had David ever once gone out of his way for her? Not that she could remember. She grinned in relief. "If you don't mind, that would be great."

The valet parking attendant pulled up in her very steady, dependable sedan and she didn't say anything when Luke took the keys, obviously intending to drive.

Surely she could give up this little bit of control? Especially when he was making such a great effort on his side.

Caryn settled into the passenger seat and was pulling the seatbelt crosswise over her body when her back spasmed again. "Oh!" she yelped before she could stop herself.

Luke reacted as if she'd screamed. "What is it? What's wrong?"

"Nothing," she hastened to assure him, regretting her outburst as she awkwardly reached around to rub her back. "I'm fine."

"You don't look fine," he said, dividing his attention between her and the road. "What if you're having some sort of premature contractions?"

She sighed. "They don't feel like contractions." The tightening in her muscles eased. "Seriously, I'm fine."

The expression on his face didn't lighten. "You need to talk to your doctor about this."

"I was just at the doctor two weeks ago. I'm not due to go back for another two weeks," she reminded him.

"Besides, the spasm is over. Between painting and dancing, I must have strained a few muscles I wasn't using before."

Luke didn't look entirely convinced. "Promise me you'll call your doctor," he repeated stubbornly.

"Why are you so worried?" she asked in an exasperated tone.

There was a long pause. "I'm not. I just don't want you to ignore any signs or symptoms of potential complications."

She arched her brow. "Potential complications?"

"The first sign of placenta previa is sharp stabbing pain," he said in a low tone. "And it could be anywhere, even your back."

She stared at him. The oddly tense expression on his face made her think the comment wasn't a random one. "Did you know someone who had placenta previa, Luke?"

He didn't answer as he pulled into her driveway.

Rather than push the issue, she gestured to her house. "Do you want to come in for a few minutes?" she offered. The sudden serious turn in the conversation made her wonder if the rest of the evening might not end as she'd hoped. "I'll make coffee."

"Sure." He climbed out, coming around to get her door. He walked her inside. "You don't have to make coffee just for me. I'll have whatever you're having."

"Herb tea." She scrunched her face in disgust. "I guess it's better than nothing."

"I'll get it." He steered her to a chair and gave a gentle push. "You need to get off your feet."

She slipped off her shoes and sighed as her toes stretched comfortably without the pressure. Did feet grow along with the rest of your body when you were pregnant? She wasn't sure.

Luke gathered cups and teabags, heating the water in the microwave. It was odd to watch him moving around her kitchen as if he belonged there. She frowned, remembering those first few days with David. David had moved in and taken over and she'd very quickly known she'd made a mistake.

Luke looked comfortable in her kitchen. In her house. In her life?

"Here you go." Luke placed a steaming mug before her, and then grabbed a second one for himself as he took a seat next to her.

She took a sip of her tea and eyed him over the rim. "Luke, you mentioned having a sister who died. Was she the one who had placenta previa?" she asked again.

He rubbed a hand over his eyes and slowly nodded. "I shouldn't have said anything. I don't want to scare you."

Too late, she thought. I'm scared. "What happened? Obstetrics wasn't my best subject but I do know a mother doesn't have to die as a result of placenta previa."

Pushing his untouched tea to the center of the table, he sighed. "Lisa was several years younger than me. I was in the second year of my residency program and trips home had almost completely fizzled out." He shrugged. "I didn't know Lisa was pregnant, she didn't tell me."

"So how did you find out?"

"My mother actually called me because Lisa suddenly

experienced severe pain and bleeding." Luke stared at his hands, reliving the past. "They'd called for an ambulance to take her to the hospital. When she got there they discovered she had a placenta previa."

Caryn knew this was when the placenta broke away from the uterine wall. She sucked in a breath. "The baby?"

"Didn't make it. And worse, after they delivered the stillborn baby Lisa continued to hemorrhage. I rushed over and they asked me to do a blood transfusion on the spot because we shared the same blood type and they were afraid she had built up antibodies in her system, which were complicating things."

Luke to the rescue. "Didn't your blood help?"

"Yeah, but I got there too late." He lifted his head, gazing at her with red-rimmed eyes full of anguish. "She died before the hospital staff had a chance to get my donated blood transfused into her. We lost Lisa and her son."

CHAPTER TWELVE

LUKE stared at Caryn's wide eyes, her arms protectively crossed over her belly, and could have kicked himself for being so thoughtless. "See? I shouldn't have said anything. A pregnant woman doesn't need to hear this. I shouldn't have upset you."

"No, it's OK." She gave him a sad smile, then stood and came around toward him. "I'm glad you told me, Luke. Sounds like you and Lisa were close."

"We were." He caught her hand and gave a tug, urging her to sit on his lap. She put her arms around his shoulders and gave him a hug.

"I'm so sorry, Luke," she said in a low tone.

He smoothed his hand over her back. "I took her death hard, almost had to repeat my second year of residency. I finally pulled it together, thanks to Mitch's help. He was my fellow while I was a resident."

She lifted her head to look at him. "I'm glad."

His heart squeezed in his chest. Caryn was so beautiful. He marveled at how perfectly she fit into his arms, rounded belly and all.

He could stay like this with her for ever.

Amazing how the very idea of spending the next hundred years with Caryn didn't scare him like it should.

When she didn't move away, he lifted a hand to cup her cheek. Holding her gaze, he leaned forward and kissed her.

She squirmed against him as if to get closer and he broke off the kiss, anxious to feel every inch of her against him. Easing her off his lap, he stood and looked down at her.

"Do all the clothes fit as nicely as this dress?" he asked in a husky tone.

"Yes." She linked her arms around his waist. "But don't even think of buying any more," she threatened in a severe tone.

"I won't." He flashed a grin. "Although there were these nightgowns…"

She blushed. "Right. As if you're desperate to see a pregnant woman's figure in a nightgown," she scoffed.

"I am." He let his gaze travel over her, gauging her reaction. He'd managed to maintain control on the dance floor at the charity ball, where all those nosy eyes could see them, but he didn't think he could walk away from her again. Not tonight. Not now. "Desperate to see you."

Her color deepened and he found her shyness enticing.

"Caryn." He drew her toward him.

"What?" her voice was breathless.

"I need another hug." I need you. I want you.

"Oh, Luke." The words were muffled because she pressed her face into his chest, locking her arms around his waist. "What are we getting ourselves into?"

He hesitated because he didn't want her to feel pressured. "Nothing you're not ready for," he said honestly. If she pushed him away, he'd go. "It's up to you. Tell me what you want."

"You," she whispered. "I want you."

His body surged with need but he kept himself under tight control as he took his time, enjoying every moment of the kiss. He'd been with other women before, but none as precious, as important as Caryn.

When he felt the edges of his control begin to disintegrate he lifted his head, gasping for breath, trying to formulate one last coherent thought. "Caryn, please, be sure."

"I am," she assured him, her lips curving in a smile. "Don't stop now, Luke."

He didn't want to stop either. When she reached down to gather the hem of her dress, as if to prove she was sure, he grasped her wrists. "Wait. Let me."

When she dropped her hands, he bent and lifted her in his arms, liking the way her body snuggled against his. Masking his underlying urgency, he asked, "Where's your bedroom?"

"Down the hall, across from the nursery." She wound her arms around his neck. "You're going to throw your back out carrying a pregnant woman around."

"Hardly." He elbowed through her door and approached the bed, then set her on her feet. He cradled her face in his hands and kissed her again.

They didn't speak as he slowly undressed her, taking his time, enjoying every moment. Her breasts were beautiful and sensitive, the merest flick of his tongue against her nipple made her gasp and press against him. As he slowly undressed her, he rid himself of his own clothing ten times faster.

He tried to be gentle but Caryn urged him on, touching him, stroking him, until he wasn't sure he could stand it another second without making her his.

She seemed momentarily surprised when he broke away to fish a condom out of his discarded jeans. Then she smiled and plucked it from him. After opening the packet, she pushed him onto his back and sheathed him. The teasing stroke of her fingers almost made him swallow his tongue.

"Now." Sweat broke out on his brow as he lifted her over him then hesitated, worried he'd somehow cause her harm. His fear was unfounded when she slid over him, taking him deep.

So good, she felt so good he couldn't stop but urged her to a quicker pace, needing to feel her release.

But she held out longer than he did, making sure he experienced the rush of pleasure before she let herself go. Blinded by a flash of white light, he momentarily forgot to breathe.

And when the quivering sensation faded and he could think clearly again, he gathered her close, tucking the blankets securely around her.

He couldn't imagine anything more perfect than falling asleep with the steady beat of Caryn's heart against his.

Caryn opened her eyes, blinking against the bright light of morning. Her first thought was how wonderful it felt to wake up beside Luke's hard muscular body. Her second thought, quickly overshadowing the first, was how she couldn't ignore the urgent pressure in her bladder. When she moved to get up, she realized Luke still had his arm wrapped protectively around her.

She smiled and disentangled herself from his embrace. This time he noticed her leaving and lifted his head, glancing around in confusion, as if trying to figure out why she was up and moving away from him.

"I need to use the bathroom." She slid from the covers, overly conscious of her nakedness as she walked across the room. She glanced over her shoulder to find Luke's keen gaze on her. "Stop staring at me."

"But I like the view." His sensual grin sent her pulse skyrocketing. "Hurry back."

She could feel her face burning as she ducked out of the room and headed for the bathroom. Thank heavens she'd left her bathrobe on the back of the door. She pulled it on gratefully.

Hiding in the bathroom wasn't her style, but now that she was awake and alone, the decisions she'd made the night before came flooding back, along with a smidgen of self-doubt.

She couldn't hide from the truth. She loved Luke. More than she'd thought possible. Luke's protectiveness was easy to understand now that she knew the story behind his sister's death. He was the complete opposite from David, as he'd proved over and over again by putting her needs first.

She finally understood her feelings for Luke, but what

exactly did he feel toward her? She buried her face in her hands. He hadn't said anything about love but he must feel something for her, the way he'd made love to her so tenderly. Maybe they should have taken things more slowly. Given themselves time. If she could get herself back on secure financial ground maybe Luke wouldn't keep seeing her as someone he needed to take care of.

"Caryn?" Luke knocked on the bathroom door. "Are you all right?"

"Fine." She stood, tightening the sash on her robe before opening the door. She found it difficult to meet his questioning gaze. "Sorry about that. Guess I'm out of practice with this sort of thing."

"Don't be sorry. Ever." His expression was serious as he leaned down to give her a quick kiss. He'd pulled on the black tuxedo slacks but not his shirt and she thought he smelt wonderful. Yet he kept things light, as if sensing her inner turmoil. "Hey, I bet baby is hungry. How about I whip together some breakfast?"

"You can cook?" She narrowed her eyes suspiciously.

"Of course I can cook breakfast. Didn't I make you tea last night?" He looped his arm around her shoulders and tucked her under his arm as they walked into the kitchen. "You just sit down there and let me show you how it's done."

Maybe he was only pampering her because of the baby, but she couldn't argue when he seemed to know what he was doing. They kept their conversation light, easy. The scent of French toast was filling the air when the doorbell pealed.

"Who could that be?" Caryn stood and made her way to the door. She groaned when she saw Debbie standing on her porch.

"Hi, Caryn. Do you have a few minutes?" Debbie wasn't smiling and by the dark circles beneath her puffy eyes she'd had a rough night.

"This isn't a good time." Caryn stayed in the doorway, unwilling to let David's sister see Luke in her kitchen at the ungodly hour of eight a.m. while she was wearing only a bathrobe.

"I'll only be a minute." Debbie's expression firmed in a stubborn line. "Please. I really need to talk to you."

How could she say no? With a sinking heart she opened the door, allowing Debbie to come in. She prayed Luke would put on his shirt, but no such luck. He came into the living room to see who was there.

"Hi, Debbie." He didn't look in the least bit embarrassed to see David's sister gaping in horror at his bare chest and bare feet. The intimacy of the situation was not lost on Debbie. "Would you care to join us for breakfast?"

"I can see why this wasn't a good time, Caryn." Debbie's eyes blazed with incredulous fury.

Her stomach clenched, furled into a knot. "I'm sorry. Please, let me explain."

Debbie went on as if she hadn't heard her. "Explain? How you're sleeping with him?" Her brittle tone sounded like she might break. "No wonder you've been visiting David less and less."

Caryn saw Luke's scowl and the way he stepped

forward on her behalf and quickly interrupted, "Luke, would you give us a few minutes alone?"

He ignored her, his gaze narrowed on Debbie. "You have no right to pass judgment on Caryn. Not when you have no idea what her relationship with David was like."

"So that's an excuse to cheat on my brother?" Debbie's voice rose sharply.

Caryn pinned Luke with a look silently telling him to shut up and blurted out, "I broke off our engagement that night, Debbie. The night before David's accident."

"How could I be so stupid?" Debbie paced in agitation, mostly talking to herself. "I should have known. You never looked at David the way you gazed at *him.*"

Stunned by Debbie's perception, Caryn sucked in a quick breath. How could she defend what was so obviously true? Caryn tried again. "Didn't you hear me? David and I had a fight. Our relationship was on the rocks and our trip to Mexico convinced me it was over. I called off the wedding."

Debbie spun toward her. "Was that before or after you got pregnant?" Then her eyes rounded. "My God. David's not the baby's father."

"That's enough!" Luke said coldly, making Caryn wince. "You're way out of line. You need to leave—now."

"Luke…" Caryn tried to get him to back off, but he wasn't listening.

"Do you have any idea what your brother put her through?" he continued in a harsh tone. "Everything he did to her?"

"Luke, stop it." Caryn glared at him, worried he was

going to reveal everything. "Debbie, please, let's talk about this."

"No, I think I've heard enough." Debbie's laugh turned into a choking sob as she shot to the door, groping blindly for the handle.

"Debbie, wait…" Caryn jerked as if she'd been slapped when the door slammed behind Debbie.

"Good riddance," Luke muttered.

A flash of red-hot fury blinded her. She rounded on him. "What is wrong with you? Why didn't you back off and leave us alone?"

"Back off?" Luke stared at her as if she'd sprouted two heads. "And let her bad-mouth you? No way. You should have told her the rest. About the drugs and the money he took from you. You should have told her everything."

"My choice, not yours." Caryn swallowed hard, feeling sick as if dozens of vitamins were playing dodgeball in her stomach. "I didn't ask you to rescue me. I could have handled this."

Luke to the rescue. The realization hit hard.

"What's wrong with me watching out for you?" he asked, truly puzzled.

"Everything. Nothing." She rubbed a weary hand over her eyes. "You don't understand, Luke. This isn't just about me. This baby is David's and my parents are gone. Doesn't my daughter deserve one set of grandparents who love her?"

"Not if they're going to hold this against you." Luke's tone was firm.

This? What? Their relationship? How could they

have a real relationship when the balance of the scale was tipped so obviously one way?

She loved Luke, but he wanted to rescue her. To take care of her.

Because she was making a mess of her life on her own.

CHAPTER THIRTEEN

LUKE heard Caryn's bedroom door close behind her with a loud click and it took all the control he possessed not to follow her. She was upset enough without him adding more to her stress. He sighed. Maybe he had been too forceful during the confrontation with Debbie.

But what had he been supposed to do? Calmly stand there and listen while David's sister whipped hateful accusations at Caryn?

Not likely.

His instinct had been to go to battle for Caryn. Defend the honor of the woman he loved.

Love. A goofy grin tugged at his mouth. He loved Caryn. With his whole heart and soul. Loved her and the child she carried. Maybe that was why he wasn't bothered by the way Debbie had assumed the baby was his. Because he'd secretly wished it was.

He walked to the hallway and glanced at Caryn's closed bedroom door, half-tempted to walk in there and demand she listen.

But the timing wasn't quite right, he realized. Bullying

his way in her bedroom wasn't the answer. He couldn't just barge in and convince her of his love. Not when she was too upset to listen.

He'd give her the time she needed to grapple with her feelings. There was no rush, they had plenty of time.

Turning on his heel, he went to the kitchen and put away the remnants of their breakfast, leaving the left-overs on a plate so Caryn could heat them up when she was ready to eat. Then he cleaned up the mess, half hoping she'd come out and give them a chance.

When there wasn't any way to stall any longer, he let himself out, walking aimlessly down the street. Caryn's house was located several miles from his, but at the moment he didn't care. A walk would be good for him. Right now, he needed to clear his head and think of a way to get through to Caryn.

Debbie's untimely arrival had ruined their magical night together. The woman's timing couldn't have been worse. He'd imagined making Caryn breakfast, then talking her back into the bedroom so they could make love again.

He frowned, remembering how Caryn had disappeared into the bathroom earlier that morning and hadn't returned for the longest time. What had been going through her mind then? Surely not doubts about how he felt about her.

No, more likely doubts about her feelings toward him. His chest tightened at the thought. Hormones had a way of messing up a person's emotions. He could certainly understand her need to be careful, to not make another mistake.

How long had it been since he'd met Caryn? He mentally counted back. A week and a half? Two weeks?

With a guilty flush he realized that the two weeks he'd known her seemed much longer. No doubt partially because of the *Crypto* crisis. Maybe he had rushed her, even though he hadn't meant to. And yet, if he had to go back and do things over again, he would still make love to her.

Because being with her felt right. There had to be a way to convince her their love wasn't a mistake.

They needed to talk. And soon. But he couldn't bulldoze his way into her heart. He had to find patience.

The woman he loved was worth the effort to make things right.

Luke called Caryn the next day to check up on her, but she didn't answer her phone. As it was Monday, he figured he'd see her in the ICU.

When he noticed Caryn wasn't anywhere around, a ripple of apprehension trickled down his spine. He found and cornered Dana. "Have you spoken to Caryn?"

"Yes, last night," Dana admitted.

"How was she?"

Dana shrugged. "She seemed fine."

Fine? He frowned. "Are you sure? Did she say anything?"

Dana rolled her eyes. "About you? No."

He ignored the pang of hurt, glancing around the unit. "Why isn't she here at work?"

"Because this isn't her scheduled day to work." Dana was growing exasperated with him. "What's with all the questions anyway? Did you guys have a fight?"

"Not exactly," he hedged. "I've left her messages, but she hasn't called me back."

"Hmm," Dana's murmur was noncommittal. "Sorry, I can't help. That's between the two of you."

Yeah. Exactly the problem. He needed a chance to prove they could make their relationship work, but what if she didn't give him that chance?

"Sorry, I have to check on my patient." Dana glanced over her shoulder where a patient's call-light was blinking. "See you later, Luke."

He nodded and glanced at his pager, which was vibrating like mad. Glad for something to do, he read the message then went down to the ED to evaluate a potential admission. As he worked, he devised a plan to drive over to Caryn's place that night after work. Much easier to talk over dinner, he concluded.

He admitted an elderly man with congestive heart failure into the ICU, wishing the nurse working alongside him was Caryn. The nurse—was her name Anna?—agreed with everything he suggested, as if she didn't have an original thought of her own.

If Caryn were here, she'd challenge him. Ask questions to make certain he was considering all aspects of a patient's comfort while providing caring support to her patient and their family.

The same way she'd supported him when he'd told her about Lisa. Coming over to hug him had been like a soothing balm to his soul. Lisa would have gotten along great with Caryn, he thought with a smile.

He liked the way he and Caryn could tease each other, yet be serious, too. The way she could lean on him, yet remain independent. The way they could laugh and very nearly cry.

Hell, who was he kidding? He loved everything about her.

Later that night, when he'd finished work, he stopped for Chinese food and headed over to Caryn's bungalow. When she came to the door, she seemed surprised to see him standing there.

"Hello, Luke."

"Hi, Caryn." She wasn't wearing the new maternity clothes he'd bought for her and his stomach dropped. Hopefully she hadn't returned them. "Are you hungry?" He held up the bag of Chinese take-out. "I brought dinner."

"I'm sorry, but I've already eaten." She didn't smile, neither did she open the door to invite him in.

He narrowed his gaze, trying to see through the screen door to the living room behind her. "Do you have a couple of minutes? I skipped lunch so I'm hungry."

She crossed her arms over her chest. "What do you want, Luke?"

Her defensive stance wasn't a good sign. "Caryn, I think we need to talk."

"Actually, I can't right now, I'm in the middle of something. Maybe another time?" The polite smile made him gnash his teeth in frustration.

He suspected there'd never be a good time.

He curled his fingers to keep from ripping the door from its hinges. "Caryn, please, let me in. Talk to me. What's going on? Why haven't you answered my calls?"

"I'm sorry, Luke, but I think it's better if we don't see each other for a while."

What? No, she didn't really mean that.

Did she?

He gripped the doorframe with both hands. "Why?" he asked bluntly. "Have you changed your mind about me? About us?"

She dropped her gaze and shrugged. "I think we jumped into things a little fast. It might be better if we step back and take this more slowly."

"OK," he agreed cautiously. "I can do slow." Hadn't he already figured that much out for himself? Patience. He needed patience. "So, then, let me ask again, would you like to have dinner? If not tonight, then tomorrow?"

She hesitated and he held his breath, fearful of her answer. Dinner was slow, wasn't it? "Tomorrow night is good," she replied after a long moment.

"Great." He forced enthusiasm into his tone. The way she didn't return his smile was not at all reassuring. "I'll pick you up at six?"

"Sounds good. See you later, Luke."

The door closed quietly in his face. He had to fight the sharp desire to break it down. Smash all the barriers standing between them once and for all.

Patience, he reminded himself as he turned and headed back to his car. Patience and perseverance would win her heart.

Because he couldn't accept the alternative.

Back at home he ate some of the Chinese food and put the leftovers in the fridge. He prowled around his apartment, almost wishing he'd volunteered to take call for the night.

He tried to catch up on his medical reading, but the walls of his condo seemed to close in around him. For a change of scenery he decided to head on over to the medical staff library.

As he searched for the latest edition of the journal put out by the Society of Critical Care Medicine, he ran into the petite dark-haired surgeon he'd met during the *Crypto* crisis, Naomi Horton.

"Hey, how are you?" she greeted him.

"Good." He smiled, gesturing to the surgical textbook she held in her hand. "What are you reading?"

"The latest techniques on cryoablation hepatic surgery," she answered on a laugh. "And you?"

"The latest comparisons of antibiotic use and septic shock." He shook his head. "Pretty sad way to spend an evening, huh?"

She laughed. "Pitiful."

The moment of silence was awkward. He didn't want to give this woman the wrong impression. As much as Naomi was nice, he longed for Caryn. He searched for a safer topic of conversation. "Did you manage to avoid drinking contaminated water?"

"Yes, thank heavens." She shifted the heavy book in her arms. "I can't believe how many of the physicians were sick. Patients, too. In fact, I have an interesting case I should ask you about. I'm wrestling with an ethical dilemma."

Work was surely a safe topic, so he glanced over to the nearby sofa. "Let's sit down, you can tell me all about it."

Naomi sat, set her book aside and tucked her dark hair behind her ears. "I was referred to this case by a rehab physician friend of mine. There's a patient in his facility who happened to get *Crypto,* which has caused his moderate kidney failure to become more severe. My friend, Dr. Lance Adams, has tried to talk the family out of dialysis because the likelihood of the patient recovering is non-existent. But so far the family has refused and, in fact, the patient's sister approached Lance, requesting to be tested as a potential kidney donor for her brother."

Luke had a bad feeling about this story. "Tell me this patient's name isn't David Morgan," he half joked.

Her eyes widened in shock. "How did you know?"

Oh, boy, it really was Caryn's former fiancé. Good grief, he could just imagine Debbie doing something so drastic as to give up her kidney for the brother who wasn't ever going to wake up.

"I know his story," he answered vaguely. "But tell me, you're not really going to test her, are you?"

"I don't know what to do," Naomi confessed. "If I refuse, I'm sure she'll just find someone else. And there is a chance she won't be a match."

"And if she is a match?" Luke asked, raising his brow skeptically. "What will you do then? Can you really follow through on a living related transplant? Surely, being severely brain-injured precludes him from being a transplant recipient?"

"It's not as if he's taking a kidney that would normally go to someone else," she argued. "I don't know—is it our right to decide what this woman does for her brother? There is that one case in a million where a person does actually recover from a severe brain injury."

"More like one chance in a billion," he muttered. "The odds of winning the lottery are better." Definitely an ethical dilemma. This must have been what Debbie had come over to talk to Caryn about the other morning. Only his presence had changed the entire focus of the conversation.

As with most ethical dilemmas, there wasn't a right or a wrong answer. He and Naomi chatted for a little while longer until he finally headed home without managing to finish his reading. So much for his usual method of losing himself in his work.

Somehow, no matter what he did, his thoughts went back on Caryn.

Outside, the spring air was cool but he was too busy wondering if he should tell Caryn about Debbie's request to notice the chilly breeze. Thank heavens she'd agreed to have dinner with him the next night. He couldn't stand the thought of not seeing her again soon.

The message light was blinking on his answering-machine. Frowning, he strode toward it and pushed the button. He'd purposefully left his pager at home since he wasn't on call and didn't want to get sucked into working at the last minute.

"Luke, this is Dana. I thought you'd want to know, I'm at the hospital with Caryn. She fell and started to hemorrhage. They're keeping her overnight in the hospital in case something happens to the baby."

Luke didn't remember driving to Trinity, but after he arrived at the hospital he nearly yanked the computer from the woman behind the information desk when she couldn't find Caryn's room fast enough. When she'd finally given him a firm destination, he rode the elevator to the eighth floor, tapping his foot impatiently as the car stopped several times on the trip up. He dashed straight to her room, barreling through the door without knocking, raking her room with a wild gaze, somewhat relieved to find her sitting up in bed, her hands cradling her stomach.

Seeing her so vulnerable robbed him of speech.

"You called him?" Caryn accused, piercing Dana with a dark scowl.

"Yes." Dana squared her shoulders, ready to take the heat. "Because I know he cares about you, Caryn."

"You shouldn't have called him," she said to Dana. "And you shouldn't have come," Caryn added in a curt tone to Luke, her gaze sliding past him. "This doesn't concern you."

"What happened?" Luke forced the words through a throat constricted with fear. She looked so tiny lying in the hospital bed. It was all he could do not to pull her close and reassure himself she was really all right.

Caryn closed her eyes as if she couldn't bear to look at him. Trying not to feel hurt by her rejection, he turned to Dana, silently demanding an explanation.

"She was painting the walls of her nursery and fell off the ladder. The spotting started a few hours later, so I brought her in."

"Has Dr. Kingsley been in to see her?" Luke asked.

"Yes. So far the baby seems fine. They plan to watch her here over night. As long as the bleeding doesn't get worse, she should be all right."

"Thank God." Dizzy with relief, he crossed over to Caryn's bed, tucking his hands in his pockets to keep from reaching for her. "Do you hurt anyplace else? Your head? Your neck? Back?"

"No." she wouldn't meet his gaze, but continued to rub her stomach in soothing circles, as if she could hold the baby in place by will alone. "A little achy maybe, but nothing serious."

He nodded, wishing there was something he could do to ease her discomfort. But she hadn't wanted him there. Wouldn't have called him, even if she'd lost the baby. The thought broadsided him with the force of a tsunami.

"Well?" Her sharp tone caught him off guard.

"Well what?" He regarded her cautiously, not wanting to mess this up like he had the confrontation with Debbie.

"Go ahead—say I told you so. This is my fault. I shouldn't have been on the ladder."

He remembered his panic the first time he'd seen her standing on it, painting the wall. If he'd had his way, she wouldn't have been anywhere near a ladder. Maybe he hadn't liked the necessity of her doing the work but he was darned if he'd give her another reason to feel guilty.

The last thing Caryn needed after the scene with Debbie was more guilt.

"No." He shook his head. "If you want to start passing around blame, then hand it over here." At her puzzled frown he continued, "I pushed you into something you weren't ready for." From the other side of the room, Dana raised an interested brow and looked as if she was trying hard not to listen. "If I hadn't interfered in your life, hadn't tried to take over, we would have painted the room together and you wouldn't have been on the ladder in the first place."

"Don't be ridiculous." Caryn's voice was heavy with exhaustion but at least she didn't seem angry any more. "You staying overnight had nothing to do with it. My ladder, my house, my problem."

He didn't know what to say to convince her otherwise. Luckily, Dana came to his rescue by changing the subject.

"Have you called David's family, Caryn?" Dana asked.

"No. It's too late tonight—I'd rather wait until the morning." He couldn't blame Caryn for putting it off. Was Dana aware of Debbie's accusations? He suspected not.

"Don't worry about it." Dana crossed over to give

Caryn a quick hug. "I have to go, I'm scheduled to work in the morning."

"Thanks for being there, Dana." Caryn returned the hug.

"You're welcome. Goodnight. See you tomorrow." Dana stood and tossed Luke a sympathetic look before leaving them alone.

"I'm staying." He leaned back in the chair and stretched his legs out.

"They're not going to let you stay," Caryn protested. "Especially when there's no reason. I'm fine."

He didn't bother arguing, because there was no way he was leaving her alone. Whether Caryn wanted to admit it or not, this wasn't something she wanted to face all by herself.

She flipped off the television and settled back against the pillows. He crossed over to turn off the overhead lights then returned to his chair beside her bed.

In the darkness he thought of all the things he wanted to say. But he'd promised to go slowly. He reached over, patting the side of the bed until he connected with her fingers. She didn't respond and he expected her to pull away, refusing even this small measure of comfort.

She didn't.

Her fingers tightened almost imperceptively around his. He brushed his thumb across the back of her hand. Closing his eyes, he let his head drop back against the chair.

The slight tangible connection was enough for now.

Plenty of time later to convince her he wasn't leaving her alone ever again.

CHAPTER FOURTEEN

CARYN hadn't expected to sleep a wink, but when she opened her eyes she realized it was already morning. She vaguely remembered the nurses coming in throughout the night to check on her but she had obviously fallen right back to sleep afterwards. Glancing over, she saw Luke was still beside her, his feet propped on the edge of her bed, his head at an awkward angle as he slept in the chair.

As promised, he'd stayed all night. Nonplussed, she stared at him. She was amazed he'd come straight over the minute Dana had called him.

Actually, she wasn't surprised. Not really. The reason she'd been upset with Dana for calling Luke had been because she'd known he'd come. She'd expected him to yell at her for being so stupid as to climb the ladder in the first place, but he hadn't. Instead, he'd tried to take the blame.

Luke to the rescue. Saving her from her own foolishness.

But had he really tried to save her this time? Thinking

back, he'd rushed into the room like a wild man, his gaze raking over her until he'd been satisfied she wasn't hurt.

In that moment he hadn't looked like a white knight riding in on his charger to save the day. Instead, he'd resembled a man flailing around for a life-preserver before he drowned. And when he'd touched her, held her hand, she hadn't pulled away.

For once it was nice to feel like she had something to offer him.

"Good morning," Marion greeted her, breaking into her troubled thoughts. The doctor's eyebrows rose when she saw Luke blinking his eyes groggily beside her. "How are you feeling, Caryn?"

"Better than yesterday," Caryn acknowledged. "No pain and no more bleeding since last night."

"Wonderful." She gave Luke a pointed glance. "I'm afraid I'll have to ask your guest to leave so I can examine you."

He stood, stretching the kinks from his neck. "Dr. Kingsley, I'm Dr. Luke Hamilton, one of the critical care fellows here at Trinity." He reached over to shake her hand.

"Nice to meet you, Dr. Hamilton." Marion smiled at him. "I hope you don't mind leaving us alone?"

"Of course not." Luke didn't argue, but turned toward Caryn. "I'll be back in a little while."

"It's not necessary for you to stay," she told him quietly. "I'm fine. I'm sure I'll be discharged soon."

"I'll be back in a little while," he repeated, turning away and heading for the door.

Stubborn man, she thought as she watched him walk away.

"Friend of yours?" Marion asked as she donned a pair of gloves.

"Yes." There was no point in denying it. Marion knew the true identity of her baby's father and, while she was sure the doctor was curious, Caryn was relieved she didn't ask any more questions.

After doing an extensive examination, Marion pronounced her healthy enough to be discharged.

"I'd like you to stay home from work for at least a few more days, just to make sure things are fine."

Caryn hid her dismay. A few days wasn't too much to ask, but she needed to make that second mortgage payment and soon. Obviously risking her baby wasn't an option so she nodded, shoving aside the worry. "I understand."

"I'll write you a note for work. If you need anything more formal, let me know." Marion washed her hands at the basin. "Don't do anything strenuous at home. And for heaven's sake, stay off the ladder."

Caryn flushed, knowing that her fall had been the result of being emotionally upset while being up on the ladder, rather than any clumsiness on her part. But she nodded again. "I will."

The door to her room opened and she glanced up, expecting Luke. But Virginia and William Morgan, David's parents, walked in.

"Caryn, how are you? How is the baby?" Virginia enveloped her in perfumed hug.

"We're both fine." Caryn's heart sank when she saw them, although their kind concern made her realize that Debbie couldn't have shared her suspicions with her parents. Debbie's absence, though, was a clear statement of how David's sister still hadn't forgiven her.

Maybe Luke was right. She should tell them the truth, especially before Debbie did.

"When your friend Dana called, we came right over," Virginia continued, her eyes full of reproach. "You should have gotten in touch with us last night."

"I didn't want you to worry over nothing." Caryn managed a weak smile even as she cursed Dana's helpfulness.

"I tried to tell Virginia that, but she doesn't listen to me." William's acerbic tone earned him a narrow glare from his wife.

"You don't listen to me either." Virginia rounded on him. "I told you I had a premonition about Caryn and the baby last night, and look what happened."

"You're always having premonitions, they rarely come true," William muttered. "For heaven's sake, Caryn and the baby are fine."

Caryn ignored their mild bickering. "Will you both, please, sit down? I have something I need to tell you." She took a deep breath and let it out slowly. "I care about you very much, and I don't want to hurt you. But the truth is, David and I broke off our engagement the night before his accident."

She braced herself for a reaction similar to Debbie's, but Virginia and William glanced at each other and then nodded. "Yes, dear. Debbie mentioned that to us," Virginia admitted.

Surprised, she stared at them. "She did? I don't understand. Aren't you upset with me?"

"Why would we be upset? You're still carrying our grandchild, aren't you?" William asked in his gruff voice.

"Yes." No matter what Debbie thought, it was the truth.

"What happened between you and David is not our business, we care about you and our grandchild," Virginia added. "Don't you know we love you like a daughter?"

Caryn waited for the familiar guilt to return, because she still hadn't told them all her secrets, but it didn't come. All she felt was relief. They didn't need to know everything else—nothing good would come of hurting David's parents with the truth.

She placed a hand over her stomach, feeling better than she had in a very long time. Free. She was finally free of the secrets. "Thanks," she murmured. "I care about both of you, too."

They exchanged a glance. "Debbie's been very upset. We've spent the night talking her out of donating a kidney to David."

Momentarily speechless, she stared at them. "Donating a kidney to David? Why?"

Virginia's smile was sad. "His kidney failure got worse after his bout with *Crypto*. I think Debbie thought she could buy him more time."

Good heavens, that must have been what Debbie had come to tell her that morning, Caryn realized. No wonder the poor woman had been upset. "Good. I'm glad you talked her out of it."

"It wasn't easy," William muttered.

Caryn glanced around, wondering where Luke was. "I guess I'd better get dressed. Dr. Kingsley is letting me go home."

"Please, take care of yourself, Caryn," Virginia said.

"I will." And she would.

"Here, we have something for you. We want you to use this money to help support the baby." William pushed a check into her hand.

"No, I can't take this." She handed it back.

"We cashed out the life-insurance policy we had on David," William said in a gruff tone. "Your son or daughter deserves it."

She didn't want to take the money, would rather dig herself out of debt on her own. Yet most of the debt wouldn't be there if not for David. And the next payment on the second mortgage was due, so she reluctantly accepted the check. The balance would be set aside in a college fund. "Thank you. Very much."

"You're welcome."

She didn't know where Luke had disappeared to, but she finally managed to convince Virginia and William she was fine. The minute they'd left, Luke strode in.

"I'll take you home," he offered.

"Were you outside my room the entire time?" she asked.

"Yeah." Luke rubbed a hand along the back of his neck. "I heard you telling them about your break-up with David. I was ready to jump in to support you if they got out of line."

She had to laugh. Typical Luke, trying to ride to her rescue. Only for some reason his actions didn't bother her so much now. Not if he allowed her to support him, too. "I didn't need your help, they're fine. I feel so much better now that they know. And they've given me a little money, plus offered to buy some things for the baby."

An odd expression filtered across his face. "Good. That's good."

"Is something wrong?" she asked.

"No. Are you ready?" Luke glanced at his watch. "I'm sorry to rush you, but Mitch is covering for me while I take you home, then I need to return to the unit."

"I'm ready—just need a minute to get dressed." Caryn refused to be disappointed by his need to get to work. Relationships were two-way streets and it was her turn to support him. His career, like hers, was important. When she emerged a few minutes later, his eyes widened in frank appreciation.

"You're wearing your new clothes," he murmured.

"Yes." She smoothed a hand over the swell of her belly in the pink clingy top. The clothes were tasteful yet trendy, and she couldn't hide how much she preferred the items Luke bought for her over Debbie's and Renee's baggy hand-me-downs. "They're beautiful."

"Only because you're the one wearing them." Luke cleared his throat and glanced away, breaking the sizzling tension. "I'll let the nurses know you're ready to go."

Caryn stoically tolerated a wheelchair ride down to

the lobby while Luke went ahead to get his car. They didn't say much on the short ride home. He insisted on escorting her into the house, and the warmth of his hand on the small of her back made her think of all kinds of things they could do in bed that weren't exactly bed-rest but was close.

"Thanks again." Settled on the sofa with a book, she smiled at him. "You'd better get to work, I'm sure Mitch is waiting."

"Yeah." He hesitated, looking as if he wanted to say more, but then he turned to leave. At her front door he paused, glanced back, his gaze enigmatic. "You're OK here alone?"

"Yes. I promised Dr. Kingsley, no more ladders."

"I'm glad." He opened the door. "I'll, uh, check on you later."

"Are you sure nothing is wrong?" She thought he was behaving oddly.

"I'm sure. Take care of yourself." He stepped outside and then closed the door softly behind him.

She bit her lip against a shaft of longing, tempted to call him back.

Was he still planning to keep their dinner plans for that evening?

As he hadn't mentioned it, she had no way of knowing for sure.

Luke did his best to concentrate on patient care, but he kept replaying the scene he'd overheard in the hospital between Caryn and David's parents over and over again.

He was glad she'd told them the truth, but listening while Caryn had taken the money they'd given her had bothered him. Not because she didn't deserve it but because selfishly he wanted to be the one to provide for her.

He wanted to marry her. Create a family with her.

Why had she insisted on taking things slowly? More than anything he wanted to rush full steam ahead, taking their relationship to the level of something more permanent.

Mitch walked into the physicians' lounge with his lunch. "I heard about Caryn. How are you holding up?"

"It was a rough night of worrying but at least she's fine now," Luke responded.

"It's scary, thinking about how fragile life is," Mitch mused. "We deal with life and death every day but when it hits at home, it can knock the foundation right out from under your feet."

"Exactly right." He knew Mitch had lost someone close to him, his son. "There's nothing worse than sitting around, feeling helpless."

Mitch raised a brow at his serious tone. "Have you finally told Caryn you're in love with her?"

"I…well…" He stopped. Because it just hit him that he'd never said the words to her. He'd never told her exactly how he felt. "Not exactly. She said she wanted to take things slowly."

"Luke, you're missing the boat here." Mitch frowned and shook his head. "Dana talks to Caryn so listen up.

She only said that bit about taking things slowly because she doesn't know how you feel about her."

"That's ridiculous." Luke couldn't believe it. "How could she not know? I've gone out of my way to show her how much I care."

"This is one of those times words would speak louder than actions," Mitch confided. "Trust me, Caryn needs to know how you really feel."

Luke replayed the scene in the hospital all over again. Spending the night next to her bed had brought them closer, but he hadn't taken advantage of that fact. Instead, all he could remember was how he'd promised to go slowly. Was Mitch right? Had she only asked him to slow down because she wasn't sure how he felt?

"All right, I'll tell her." Luke thought for a minute. "I think there's a way I can show her and tell her how I feel at the same time."

Bed-rest sounded good until you were forced to stay in your house, staring at the four walls around you without doing a thing to fix or clean all the things that suddenly, glaringly needed immediate attention.

As the hour grew later, she told herself not to get her hopes up that Luke would honor their dinner date. But lecturing herself didn't make her any less hopeful every time she heard a car drive down the street.

At half past six, she got up and headed into the kitchen to make something easy for dinner.

Dr. Kingsley had indicated she could do simple things, like walk to the kitchen to make herself meals and walk to the bathroom for showers, but anything more strenuous was out of the picture for a couple of days.

Making herself a peanut-butter and jelly sandwich, she wallowed for a moment in self-pity.

The baby kicked, hard, as if protesting her thoughts.

"Hey, you're not old enough to have your own opinion," she joked, smoothing the spot on her belly where the baby had kicked. Then she laughed at herself. "Maybe you're right. I am being stupid. I should just call Luke and ask him to come over."

Before she could make the first move, her phone rang. She pounced on it. "Hello?"

"Caryn?" She immediately recognized Luke's voice. "How are you?"

"Fine. Great." She forced cheerfulness into her tone. "The baby's kicking like a soccer player."

"Guess she's back to her usual active self, huh?"

"Absolutely." Caryn heard the beeping of monitor alarms in the background and wondered how things were going in the ICU. It seemed as if she hadn't been there much since the *Crypto* crisis. "Are you still at work?"

"Yeah, there was a little crisis earlier but I'm leaving now." He cleared his throat. "I'd like to stop by and see you."

Yes! She wanted to shout and punch the air with her fist but she refrained. Her heart thudded loudly in her chest and she struggled to keep her voice even. "That would be nice."

"Good, I'll see you soon." He hung up before she could respond.

He hadn't forgotten. There was a crisis at work. A patient taking a sudden turn for the worse must have caused him to stay late. *He hadn't forgotten.*

She went into the bathroom to touch up her make-up. Just because she was pregnant it didn't mean she couldn't look her best.

When Luke had stopped by the other night with Chinese food, he'd wanted to talk but she hadn't let him.

Tonight they really did need to talk.

She flipped through a few television channels but couldn't find anything that captured her interest. After checking her watch for the eleventh time in as many minutes, she picked a channel and stayed with it, although after ten minutes she couldn't have described what she'd watched.

When Luke knocked, she almost leapt off the sofa to answer the door.

"Hi." She couldn't hide her pleasure at seeing him.

"Hi, yourself." He stepped forward and swung her into his arms in a move so quick she gasped.

"What are you doing?" she asked, clinging to his broad shoulders with a reflexive grip. "Giving yourself a hernia?"

"You're not supposed to be on your feet." When he turned and headed out of her house down the sidewalk toward the street, she saw it. A beautiful white horse-drawn carriage, complete with a driver wearing a shiny tall black hat.

"Luke?" She peered up at him, wondering if she was

imagining the sight. Curious, she glanced around but there wasn't anyone else striding toward the fancy white carriage. "What did you do?"

"I arranged for a carriage ride." He stood patiently holding her as the driver climbed down to open the door. He gently set her on the cushioned seat.

Amazed, she could only gape at him in shock. "You did?"

He nodded. Awestruck, she slid over to make room for him as he climbed in beside her. Curious, she glanced around. The top of the carriage had been pulled up as protection against the wind and there were tiny lights along the rim. Inside, the seat was soft crushed velvet, she thought was red but it was difficult to tell in the darkness.

The driver didn't say a thing but simply got into his seat and clucked to the horse. The carriage gave a little jerk as the horse began to walk with a clackety-clack of hooves on the pavement.

Caryn settled back against the cushions, enjoying the quiet ride. The night was clear and mild, although there was a lap blanket provided for warmth. Luke put his arm around her and drew her close. Giving in to the desperate need to touch him, to smell the familiar musky, protective scent of him, she leaned against him.

"This is a wonderful surprise, Luke," she murmured. "I've never in my life been on a carriage ride."

"I'm glad." He took her hand and stared down at it for a moment. "Caryn, I know things have been difficult lately, first your pregnancy, then the *Crypto* outbreak, then dealing with Debbie, then your fall…"

She winced and placed a protect hand over her stomach. "Don't remind me."

"But there's something I want you to know," Luke continued as if she hadn't interrupted. "I love you. I love you and your baby." He put his hand into his pocket, pulled out a small velvet case and opened it with a flick of his thumb, revealing a large diamond. He held it out for her. "Will you marry me?"

"Oh, boy," she whispered, flabbergasted by the sparkling diamond he'd presented. She hadn't expected this. She really, really hadn't expected this. They were supposed to talk. "Oh, Luke." She curled her fingers into fists, digging her nails into her palms to keep from taking the ring. "I don't know what to say."

He nodded, not in the least bit put off by her less-than-enthusiastic response. "I know you planned to raise your child alone, that you don't need me because you have David's parents' financial and emotional support. But I'm asking you to reconsider." He paused, and then added, "I think your baby deserves a complete family."

Her frisson of excitement faded. "Is that the only reason you want to marry me, Luke? Because of the baby?"

"No. I love you, Caryn."

She wanted to believe him. But then she remembered his white-knight routine and wondered if he realized the truth himself. "Maybe you don't. Maybe you just want to save me from myself."

"Save you?" He laughed. "Caryn, you're the one who saved me. I was attracted to you from the start, but the more I got to know you, the more I wanted to be with you." His smile was crooked. "Your caring concern toward Mrs. Nowicki's son made me realize what I was missing from life."

Hope fluttered, swelled. "You need to be sure, Luke, because I don't want you to see me as someone who needs to be rescued."

He shook his head. "I don't see you like that at all. I've never met anyone as strong as you, Caryn." He reached over to place his hand protectively on the swell of her abdomen. "But I can't deny I feel protective about you and your baby. I hadn't really thought about what it would be like to be a father until I met you."

He looked so serious she couldn't help but believe he really meant it. "You might not feel the same way when the baby is crying in the middle of the night and we're both tired and crabby," she warned. "Not only that, but it's complicated. This baby is going to need her grandparents as much as her grandparents are going to need her."

He stared down at the ring. "I know it's not going to be easy, but nothing worthwhile ever is."

Humbled, she stared at him.

"This baby is important to me, Caryn. I understand she's David's daughter and, of course, her grandparents will remain a part of her life. But I hope you'll allow her to be my daughter, too."

Love intertwined with threads of hope bloomed in her chest, making tears dampen her eyes. She swiped them away with the back of her hand and sniffled. "I think she'll like that."

He cradled her cheek. "And how does her mother feel?"

"Her mother likes that, too." Half laughing, half crying, she threw her arms around his neck and pulled him close. "I love you, Luke. I love you so much. I was stupid to doubt your feelings."

"Not stupid. Smart. Cautious. Beautiful. Sexy." Covering her mouth with his, he kissed her, drawing her legs over his lap so he could reach her more fully.

"Giddyap!" The driver called out to the white horse.

Pulling away from Luke, she realized they'd passed the park located a few blocks from her house for the second time. "I think the driver is going in circles," she whispered. "Is he lost?"

He laughed. "I don't care if he's lost. He can drive in circles all night, if that's what it takes to make you happy."

"I don't need a diamond ring or a fancy carriage ride to make me happy," she told him seriously. "I only need you."

"I know. I need you, too." Luke took the ring from the velvet box and slipped it on her finger. "That's just another reason why I love you, Caryn. Because all my life I've been looking for someone exactly like you."

EPILOGUE

"Come on, Caryn. Push. You can do this," Luke encouraged, trying to remain calm, although watching her suffer through the agonizing pain was killing him. Nightmares of the night he'd lost Lisa had haunted him as Caryn's delivery date loomed closer. He'd promised to be here for her.

And he would be. No matter what.

Sweat dampened the hair at her temples and stained her hospital gown, and the muscles in her neck corded as she clutched his hand, straining to push.

"That's it, almost finished. See the head? Let's suction out the mouth, now the shoulders—there! Congratulations, Caryn and Luke. You have a beautiful baby girl."

Luke nearly wept with relief as the baby began to cry. While the hospital staff did a quick apgar score, he kissed his wife. He couldn't think of a better way to celebrate their three-month wedding anniversary. "A girl. Did you hear that, Caryn? You were right all along. We have a beautiful baby girl."

"Seven pounds even and twenty inches long. Here, you can hold her now." Marion wrapped the baby in a pink blanket and placed her in Caryn's waiting arms.

"Oh, Luke. Isn't she wonderful?" Caryn kissed the baby's soft crown.

"Yes. Almost as beautiful as you." Luke couldn't believe his good fortune to have two precious women in his life. As he stared down at their tiny daughter, he vowed to be the best husband and father he could possibly be.

"Her fingers are so slender and dainty." Caryn gazed up at him with shiny eyes. "Maybe she'll be a pianist."

He had to laugh. "Not a surgeon?"

She giggled. "Of course! What was I thinking?"

Glancing over to the doorway, he figured it was time to let the rest of the family see the newest addition. Caryn held up the pink bundle and he gently took the baby into his arms. They'd already decided on names. For a girl they'd chosen a first name in memory of Caryn's mother Loraine, and in memory of her biological father they'd decided to use David's surname as the baby's middle name.

The last name would be Luke's.

He walked out to the hallway, where the rest of the family was waiting. Everyone was there—David's sisters and brothers, David's parents, and even his mother, along with her latest husband. Proudly he held up the baby for all to see.

"Caryn and I would like to introduce our daughter, Raine Morgan Hamilton."

By the enthusiastic response from the room, Luke was satisfied his daughter would always be surrounded with love.

And love was the secret to a lifetime of happiness.

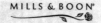

MILLS & BOON®   0407/03b

_MedicaL
romance™

HIS RUNAWAY NURSE
by Meredith Webber

Twelve years after her sudden departure, Flynn can't believe his eyes when Majella Goldsworthy returns. She is nothing like the girl he once knew and now has a three-year-old daughter. Majella has come home to forge an independent life for herself and little Grace, but Flynn soon finds himself wondering if there could be room for one more in this very special family.

THE RESCUE DOCTOR'S BABY MIRACLE
by Dianne Drake

When Dr Gideon Merrill finds out Dr Lorna Preston is coming to film his search-and-rescue operation in a storm-devastated Brazilian village, everything about their failed marriage comes flooding back. But a night of passion changes everything and soon Gideon realises that he and Lorna have made a tiny miracle of their own...

EMERGENCY AT RIVERSIDE HOSPITAL
by Joanna Neil

Dr Kayleigh Byford has had enough of men – no matter how promising they start out, they always let her down. Her return to her home town has already had enough complications – the last thing she needs is another distraction in the form of Lewis McAllister, her seriously gorgeous boss at Riverside A&E!

On sale 4th May 2007

Available at WHSmith, Tesco, ASDA, and all good bookshops
www.millsandboon.co.uk

4 FREE

BOOKS AND A SURPRISE GIFT!

We would like to take this opportunity to thank you for reading this Mills & Boon® book by offering you the chance to take FOUR more specially selected titles from the Medical Romance™ series absolutely FREE! We're also making this offer to introduce you to the benefits of the Mills & Boon® Reader Service™—

- ★ FREE home delivery
- ★ FREE gifts and competitions
- ★ FREE monthly Newsletter
- ★ Exclusive Reader Service offers
- ★ Books available before they're in the shops

Accepting these FREE books and gift places you under no obligation to buy, you may cancel at any time, even after receiving your free shipment. Simply complete your details below and return the entire page to the address below. You don't even need a stamp!

YES! Please send me 4 free Medical Romance books and a surprise gift. I understand that unless you hear from me, I will receive 6 superb new titles every month for just £2.89 each, postage and packing free. I am under no obligation to purchase any books and may cancel my subscription at any time. The free books and gift will be mine to keep in any case.

M7ZED

Ms/Mrs/Miss/Mr ....Initials ....

BLOCK CAPITALS PLEASE

Surname ....

Address ....

....

....Postcode..................................

Send this whole page to:
UK: FREEPOST CN8I, Croydon, CR9 3WZ